Explicit Demands

Viktor Redreich

Redreich Publishing Limited

Free Book

Get your free book now

https://redreich.com/dirtysecrets

Published by Redreich Publishing Limited

71-75 Shelton Street, Covent Garden London WC2H 9JQ United Kingdom

Contents

Chapter One

Eyes up here, creep!

THE FAMILIAR FEELING OF watchful eyes gazing at her warmed Kate's skin. It was just as she liked it: all of the attention on her. A little thrill went down her spine, sending sparks flying through her back and shoulders.

There was no better feeling in the world, especially when all the eyes on her were male. Kate made it no secret that she loved teasing men. Toying with their emotions, playing them off one another, taunting them like they were in a schoolyard. It pleased her to no end.

Kate wasn't the kind of woman to take shit from anyone—especially not a man. She'd endured enough of their bull for one lifetime and she wasn't about to lie on her back and take more.

She rolled her shoulders in their sockets as she looked down at the laptop placed on the table in front of her. It was plugged in and ready to go. The projector next to the laptop beamed onto the wall behind, the bright blue light blinding. The speech she'd prepared was placed on the table in front of her, the text printed big enough for her to see from where she stood.

All she had to do was start speaking. But something stopped her from opening her mouth. Whispers were emanating from the far end of the room. Kate's dark blue eyes flicked over to the sight of their mouths moving, their ugly smug smiles curving up in the corners, making their cheeks wrinkle.

It was the ultimate sign of disrespect. Every single person in this room demanded silence when they made their presentations. So why wasn't she given the same?

Kate glanced around at all the faces sitting around the large, oval table. All of the men sat there, waiting with expectant looks on their faces. She knew, without a doubt, that none of them cared enough to hear her opinion. They were courteous enough to sit silently and pretend they were listening, however.

All of them aside from those jerks at the end. They were still whispering away like school children, breaking out into gentle fits of laughter. Kate wasn't going to start speaking until they stopped, she'd decided. They would have never behaved this way to a male colleague. Why should she accept any less?

"Is there a problem?" A voice called out from two seats away from her.

Kate looked at him. It was Walter Harpe, the Vice President of Production. Technically, he was her boss. His hair was all gray and white, almost translucent in the right light, and his face was covered in deep-set wrinkles and age spots. He was old, older than she could have guessed, and yet he was still working.

"If I could have everyone's attention," Kate said bluntly.

Walter looked behind him, at the two men whispering, before turning back around in his seat. "You have it."

He was wrong. The two men hadn't stopped talking. Kate stared at them, feeling the anger rising in her stomach, causing it to bubble and sizzle. Both of the men had dark brown hair and equally dark eyes. Their cheeks were plump and cleanly shaven. They looked average for middle-aged men.

The suits on their bodies were expensive, but both their cuts were atrocious. Clearly, the suits had been made years ago, when the men had been a little lighter around the waist. Their rotund, fatty stomachs poked out of the bottom of their jackets, their shirts barely able to stay tucked into their pants.

"I'm not going to start without everyone's undivided attention," Kate stated.

She wasn't going to let them talk over her for the entire meeting. Weeks of her time had been spent on this presentation. Having two men talking over her wasn't in the cards, not for Kate.

Begrudgingly, the men ended their conversation with mutters of *we'll finish this later*. Their bodies turned to face her, their smug smiles vanished from their lips.

"Thank you," Kate said sharply.

She leaned down to her laptop and put the presentation on full screen. The projector lit up in a brighter shade of blue, taking up the whole wall behind her.

“As you all know, those in the TV department have been working alongside the designers to come up with a brand new, sleek design for our Metadynamic and Twentyfour-K ranges,” Kate started. “Our main goal was to find a way to bring down the price of our range to compete with what is currently on the market.”

Kate leaned down and pressed a button on her laptop, switching to the next slide. Behind her were now pictures of dozens of different models from different manufacturers, all labeled with price, design pros and cons, and reviews from top technology influencers.

It was clear to most in the room that Kate had done the research. A lot of the men leaned forward in their seats to read the smaller pieces of text, nodding as they absorbed everything she was showing them.

“As you can see, our products are over-priced compared to what else is on the market,” she said. “So, to improve sales and our brand, we’re trying to bring our costs down without using inferior components or substandard design.”

A lot of the men in front of her had no idea about TVs. They were the big boys from corporate. They allocated the funds and approved projects, but they didn’t know the details, and they often didn’t care for them. All they needed to know was if they were going to make money—and Kate had made sure to use that knowledge to her advantage.

"So far, a lot of the Twentyfour-K TVs on the market are clunky with unintuitive features," Kate continued. "We're aiming to streamline the design and bring the price down so average consumers can have the technology in their homes."

She leaned forward once more, pressed the button on her laptop, and moved to the next slide. As she stood up, her eyes flicked to the end of the table where she saw movement. The two men had come together, their heads almost touching as they spoke quietly to one another.

Kate's blood ran cold in her body as she straightened up, staring at them without blinking. She watched their lips moving as they whispered. There was no way she was going to continue. Having to tell two, fully grown men to shut up was absolutely ridiculous.

Instead of saying something straight away, Kate decided to keep it petty and clear her throat loudly. She felt her vocal cords slap together as she made the noise, staring the men down.

Both of them looked up to her immediately and nodded for her to continue, but they didn't separate themselves and sit up properly. Kate eyed them, knowing that they were going to start talking again when they thought they were in the clear.

"As I was saying," Kate said, hearing the anger seep through in her own voice. "Our departments have been working really hard on some of these early designs."

She pressed the button again, switching the slide. A sketch appeared on the wall behind her, bright and white. It was an early drawing showing how they were planning to scale all of the technology down, making it smaller and more lightweight than ever before.

"And this is all doable?" Walter asked, leaning forward in his chair, his elbows placed on the edge of the table. "You're sure?"

"I wouldn't bring it to the board if it wasn't," Kate snapped. "My teams have assured me that this design will work."

A couple of the men glanced at each other. Clearly, none of them could believe that she'd done the work and calculations, or had her team even double-check that it was plausible. Doubting a woman was second nature to them. It came so naturally, that they didn't even think about it.

Kate could have screamed as she watched the men sitting in front of her, actively doubting her as they glanced between themselves. Just open her mouth and let all of the rage fly out. That wouldn't solve anything, though. And it would just reinforce the idea that women were irrational and over-emotional.

She had to keep herself composed and calm. If not for herself, then for the rest of the women in the company. An example needed to be set and it started here, in the board meeting.

"Anyway," she said, trying to remain calm, "moving onto the technical specifications."

That was all it took for the two men to start talking again. They weren't going to stop. According to them, she didn't deserve their silence. Kate balled up her fists as she stared at their pudgy faces, feeling the hatred rising inside of her.

This is why I'm still single, she thought bitterly. *Men think women are nothing. They think we're worthless.*

The thoughts didn't help Kate keep a cool mind. She felt her lips parting as the anger came rushing up her throat like vomit.

"Stop talking," she said forcefully, raising her voice without meaning to. "Show me the respect I deserve and pay attention to what I have to say."

She had everyone's attention after that. Some of the men gawked at her, their mouths falling open in shock. Kate wanted to roll her eyes into the back of her skull. How pathetic they all were, shocked that a woman would dare speak to them in such a manner.

"Excuse me?" One of the talkers asked, chortling. "Did you really just speak to me like that?"

"I did," Kate snapped. "Do you not realize how rude you're being? Mr. Harpe already asked you to shut up. Why didn't you listen?"

The man narrowed his eyes and stood out of his seat, shaking his head slowly. "I won't be spoken to like this," he snapped. "This is outrageous."

"So was your behavior," Kate replied. "You can sit quietly and listen to me for thirty minutes. It's not hard. Somehow you manage to do it for all of the male colleagues present. Why am I worth talking over while they're not?"

The man put his hands on his hips and scoffed as he stared around the room. It was like he couldn't believe that a woman had dared to call him out on his asshole behavior. Kate just stood at the head of the table, expectant.

"Too scared to answer?" Kate goaded him.

"Of course, the *woman* makes it about sex," the man scoffed. "You women always make it about what's between your legs."

"Maybe if you'd listened to me it wouldn't have come to this," Kate replied. "I don't see what's so important that you had to talk over me for almost the entire time."

It was clear he wasn't going to answer Kate. He just kept looking around at his colleagues, expecting someone to come to his rescue. When no one did, he stormed away from the table and went for the door. With his hand gripping the handle, he looked back to the room and raised his eyebrows as if to say *well?*

Kate stared him down, unwavering. She wasn't going to apologize for asking for respect. She wasn't going to apologize for calling him out on his bullshit. After all, he'd be one of the first people to call her out if she dared pull the same crap.

"This is information that you all asked for," Kate continued. "You asked me to make this presentation. You asked me to provide this information. Why the hell should I be talked over when I'm giving you exactly what you asked for?"

"You can't police us," one of the men in the back replied.

His black hair was scattered with stripes of gray, thinning at the top. His face was fairly wrinkle-free but Kate couldn't really tell. He had a thick, dark beard covering the bottom half of his face and most of his neck.

"And yet if I ever dared to talk over any of you, I'd be thrown out of the meeting," Kate said. "This is disgusting and I can't believe this has escalated because one man couldn't keep his trap shut."

Kate stared over at him, his face dark and shadowed with rage. She knew she'd gone a step too far. Not only had she called him out, but now she'd embarrassed him in front of his colleagues. People he had to see every day. People he dealt with regularly.

Of course, she didn't give a shit about his feelings, but she did care about her job. Without it, she'd be nothing. She loved her job. She lived for it. She'd spent years climbing her way to the top, using everything in her toolbox to get herself into power. And now she was here, she was starting to think it wasn't everything she'd expected it to be.

Kate had always assumed that when she got to the top, she'd be taken seriously. She always thought that those powerful, working women didn't have to put up with sexist crap.

Clearly, it still mattered, but those women were hard working and didn't let the men around them get in the way. Kate wasn't sure if she could be like that. How could she let words roll off her back like they meant nothing? That wasn't a skill she had.

Walter stood up from his seat slowly, his old stiff joints giving him trouble. He groaned and sighed as he tried to balance himself. When he was finally standing, he began to move over to Kate.

She watched him carefully. His coming over to her wasn't going to be anything good. Out of all of them, Walter was the worst. Kate couldn't count how many times he'd told her that the office wasn't the place for a woman. Just his presence irked her.

As he approached, Kate saw that his arm was reaching out for her, aiming right for her shoulders. Before she could move away, she felt

Walter's arm over her shoulders, his hand winding around her back to hold onto her upper arm.

"I think what Kate was trying to say," he started, giving her arm a gentle squeeze, "is that she'd like it if people listen to her while she speaks."

"That's exactly what I said, Walter," Kate said, feeling the anger rising up her throat like bile.

"Well, I think Kate needs to work on her communication skills," Walter said with a patronizing, happy tone in his voice. "How about you leave your presentation here, go and cool down for a little while, and we'll continue on without you?"

Kate shrugged off his old, wrinkly arm and stepped away from him. The projector beamed onto her body, blinding her from the rest of the room.

"Are you kidding me?" Kate asked. "I worked on this for weeks and now you're going to take it away from me and take all the credit yourselves because some asshole couldn't keep his fucking mouth shut?"

Kate moved to her laptop and slammed the lid closed before yanking out all of the cables. She clutched it under her arm as she stared at her boss, the anger seeping out of her skin and into the air around her.

"Absolutely not," she said. "If a man was standing here, giving this presentation, the whole fucking room would be silent. And you all know it. But none of you believe that a woman has anything worthwhile to say and that's why you're all allowed to speak over me. And that's why I'm being punished for speaking out against it. You're all fucking assholes."

As soon as Kate had closed her mouth, she knew that she'd fucked up. Why the hell did she think that it was okay to talk to her boss like that? Or the other men in the room? They were all higher in the company than her, and their delicate male egos weren't going to let her get away with this.

She was too embarrassed to take a quick look around the room but, out of the corner of her eye, she could see the men shifting uncomfortably in their seats.

Damnit, Kate thought. *Damnit, damnit, damnit.*

"Kate," Walter said sharply. "I'm going to need to talk to you outside. Now."

Chapter Two

Red hot

THE ANGER HAD TAKEN over her whole body. Kate could barely control herself as she stormed into her house. She kicked the front door shut so hard it made the whole front of the house shiver. If she'd been bothered to glance back at the door, she'd have seen the black outline of her high-heeled shoes in the paint.

Once she had kicked off her shoes, watching them as they flew across the hallway in front of her, she tried to steady her ragged breaths. Bare-footed, she stood in the middle of the hallway as she stroked her free hand through her hair.

Her golden rings got stuck in her knotted locks but that wasn't going to stop her. She continued raking her fingers down her head, trying to see through the red fog that had fallen over her eyes.

It wasn't easy for her to see through the fog, let alone breathe. Her lungs were burning from the deep breaths she was taking and large, black and red spots were clouding her vision.

Kate set her laptop on the side table beside her, not angry enough to smash it yet, and stumbled through her home. The rage was in every inch of her, turning her legs to jelly and making her stomach cramp painfully.

The living room was immediately to her right, filled with cream couches and brightly colored cushions. She roamed through it, her feet padding loudly against the dark wood floor below, as she made her way to the back of the house where the kitchen was.

All she wanted was a glass of water. Ice water. That was it. It would cool her down and give her a chance to regain herself. There was so much pent-up anger inside of her body that she was afraid her heart might explode.

Her hand reached up and slapped against her chest, sending a wave of vibrations through her rib cage. Beneath her palm, she could feel her heart thundering inside her. The blood was rushing through her veins, helping the adrenaline flow through her.

It felt like it would never stop. Her hands shook as she reached for the refrigerator and clutched onto the handle of the glass jug of water. As she brought it out into the warm air of her house, the glass turned cloudy.

When she had a glass of water in her hand, bringing it to her lips to sip at it, she let her finger slide across the glass jug. The cold condensation chilled her finger to the bone. For a moment, it felt like she was calming down.

The water slipped down her throat, cooling her down to her very core. Kate tried to clear her head as the water went down but the memories continued to pulse behind her eyes.

The way Walter had put his arm around her shoulders, the way the men had talked over her so openly, the way that they had disrespected her day in and day out. Kate's stomach clenched and her teeth gritted together. Her fingers around the glass gripped harder, making her whole arm shake under the strain.

They wouldn't have been so rude to me if I were a man, she thought bitterly, staring down at the jug in front of her. *They're so obsessed with what's between my legs that they can't concentrate on what's coming out of my mouth.*

Kate tried not to think about it, tried to push it from her mind, but the images just kept coming back. She could still feel Walter's arm over her shoulder, his hand gently squeezing her. Kate rolled her shoulder as if she were trying to get Walter's hand off her once more, and a shudder went through her body.

"Why are all men so obsessed with their cocks?" Kate shouted the last word, letting it burst out of her mouth and echo around the empty room.

She set her glass on the counter, next to the jug, and put both of her palms on the counter. As she breathed deeply, she leaned her body forward and let her head hang loosely between her arms. She stayed like that for a while, trying to center herself. The rage was controlling her, making her angrier than she needed to be, and she knew she had to get it under control. If she didn't, she'd just be stuck as a raging bitch for the whole day.

A long, loud scream came out of her mouth, turning her voice instantly raw with the veracity of it. It went on and on, a never-ending *fuuuuuuuuuck!* that could probably have been heard for miles around her home.

Kate didn't care what other people thought of her, though. All she knew was what she needed, what she had to do for herself to keep her head above water. And this wasn't it. Tolerating Walter, the board of directors, all of them. It was bullshit.

Their sexism was eroding away at her mental health, taking her to the breaking point. There was no way she would be able to handle this for much longer.

Well, I do have a month to myself now, Kate thought as she stood up straight, her tired red eyes gazing around her empty kitchen.

Just thinking about taking a week off terrified Kate. She'd not been on vacation for as long as she could remember. It wasn't that she didn't have the money for it—because she did, she had more than enough of that—but it was the fact that she could so easily be replaced.

How many men were there, looking to get into the higher rankings of her job? How many men would love to be the head of a department in a huge electronics brand? There were so many qualified men underneath her, in her own company, constantly vying to get her job.

They would try to discredit her, to show her bosses that she was inferior because she had a vulva between her goddamn legs, but she'd always managed to clap back and show them who was boss. Kate was the boss... or, at least, she had been.

What was she going to go back to, after this month-long vacation? She couldn't be sure of that. Someone was going to have to step in for her and it was probably going to be a man.

A man that would have the same ideas as her, the same vision, only *he* would be listened to and therefore rewarded for his insight. There was no doubt in her mind that the man would have the same insight as she'd had. Maybe even inferior insight. But he'd be regarded as a hero of the department.

Fuck, no, Kate thought, squeezing her eyes shut. *I can't think about this. I'm going to have a fucking heart attack.*

Instead of focusing on the things she was going to miss at work, she tried to think about what she was going to do with her newfound freedom. To Kate, it was like finding a huge pot of gold.

As she moved out of the kitchen, she tried to think about what *normal* people did when they had time off: they went on vacations, relaxed, and didn't think about work.

That wasn't possible for her, though. She'd spent her whole life working hard to get to where she was. She wasn't about to just forget about it for a month. If she was going to relax and enjoy her time, she was going to have to find an activity to do that would enable her to stay up to date with work.

Spying on the emails would be the easiest way. No one would see that she was reading them and, by office protocol, she would still be CC'd in. So all she needed to do was make sure she had internet access and she'd be fine.

In theory. Kate went into the hallway to get her laptop, wondering if anyone had started gossiping about her over emails. Of course, she doubted it, and if they did they would at least be smart enough to remove her from the CC. Or were they?

Kate put her laptop on the breakfast bar in the kitchen and sat on the high stools as she waited for it to boot. The anger was still inside her, trying to bubble up and come out of her mouth, but she wasn't going to let it. She'd somehow gotten control of her emotions and that was exactly how it was going to stay.

If she let herself scream and shout and rant and rave and curse the heavens for everything that happened, she knew she wouldn't be able to get anything meaningful done. She'd just hole up in her bedroom and sob the month away.

That wasn't the kind of person she wanted to be. That wasn't the kind of woman she wanted the world to see when they looked at her. She wanted to be robust, strong, and independent. A force to be reckoned with. None of those things meant crying in bed all day.

Kate scrolled through her emails but nothing there was out of the ordinary. There wasn't any mention of her being out of the office for the next month, so Kate knew that they had probably put out a bulletin on the computer system for her team to see.

How embarrassing, Kate thought.

The idea that her colleagues were wondering about what happened in the meeting set her teeth on edge. No doubt they were going to assume that she'd fucked everything up and now they didn't have a plan going forwards.

That wasn't true, though. Sure, Walter forced her to take a month-long vacation to *relax, reset, and unwind*. But that didn't mean she was going to forget the progress her team had made. As soon as she got back to work, she knew she was going to reschedule that meeting.

Kate paused scrolling as she thought. *What if the same thing happens? What if I get talked over? What if more people do it? Will I lose my shit and get fired?*

That was completely and totally out of the question. She'd worked herself into the ground to get to where she was, fighting the male ego and bureaucracy, all the way to the top.

There was nothing else for Kate to do but close down her email program. Torturing herself wasn't going to do anything besides make her more unstable. She needed to take Walter's words to heart. Relax, reset, and unwind. That was her job for the next month. That was what she needed to focus on.

As Kate went to close her laptop, she hoped that her job would still be waiting for her when she returned. Her palm rested against the top rim of the screen as she stared at her background picture: it was grainy and frayed at the edges where she'd scanned the terribly old picture. Kate had to be only eighteen in it. Her mother was standing beside her, her long, blonde, curly hair falling down to her shoulders in thick, luscious waves.

Kate thought about going to see her mom. It had only been a couple of weeks since they saw each other, but it was always nice to have mom and daughter time... right?

The front door opened. The sound of it drew Kate out of her mind, her eyes darting over to the opening door. There, with a bag slung over her shoulder and the keys lodged in the door, was Claire.

She was only eighteen, such a young precious thing. Kate smiled widely, beaming as she looked at her daughter. Just like Kate's mom, Claire had long, curly blonde hair. Somehow the genes had skipped Kate and gone to Claire instead.

Even Claire's face looked like her mom's. She had a wide jaw that made her look like a model, with eyes that were just a little farther apart than the normal population. In the middle of her face, she had a beautiful ski-sledge nose that belonged to Claire's father.

Kate hated that she could see him in Claire. She loved her daughter's face—and she loved her daughter—but the constant reminder of *him* there was unnerving. The fucker had abandoned them when Claire was only five years old. Why did he get to be a part of her when he chose to leave them behind?

Claire looked up to her mother, her dark blue eyes glittering amongst the deep freckles she'd accumulated over the summer break.

"Why are you home so early?"

What a greeting, Kate thought. *No "hey, how's your day mom?"*

Kate closed her laptop and forced a smile onto her lips as she turned in the seat to face her daughter properly. "I'm going to take a vacation," she said, trying to make it sound like her idea.

Claire dropped her bag onto the floor, a shocked look in her eyes. "Who's making you take a vacation?"

"No one," Kate laughed. "I thought it would be good for me."

Claire just stared at Kate, her face clearly unamused.

"My boss," Kate sighed. "He thinks it will be good for me and... I agree."

The last words out of her mouth sounded pained, even to her own ears. She grimaced as she turned around in the seat, leaning into the back. Kate folded her arms across her chest and shook her head from side to side, ever so slowly.

"What a fucking joke," Kate mumbled.

"So, you're not fired?" Claire asked.

Kate could only shake her head in reply. The words swimming around her head haunted her: *not yet, not yet, not yet.*

"I'm going to go and meet a friend," Claire said, sounding uneasy. "Are you going to be okay?"

Kate forced a smile onto her lips once again. "Sure, sweetie," she said. "You have fun with your friend."

That wasn't exactly true, though, was it? Kate had been monitoring her daughter's phone for years. She had to. Ever since she'd found her daughter sitting inappropriately on her piano teacher's lap, she'd had to have some control over the situation.

Claire was a lovely girl, there was no denying that, but she had issues with men. All because of her good-for-nothing father. If he hadn't abandoned them, Kate knew that all of this would be non-existent.

But no. He had to be selfish. He forced Kate to work herself half to death just to keep up with the middle-class lifestyle Claire deserved. And with two absent parents, that meant that Claire was raised by nannies and tutors.

And now her daughter was having an affair with a married man, twice her age. The thought of it made Kate's skin crawl. But what could she do? Force Claire to stop seeing him? Kate wasn't even supposed to know about it. The only reason she knew was because she'd seen the dirty texts Claire had been sending him.

Of course, Kate had looked the guy up to find out who he was. That's how she'd known he was married. A very rich, very married man. The fact that Claire could do that to another woman disgusted her, but she couldn't bring it up. She just had to pretend like nothing was wrong and hope to hell her daughter saw sense.

Aside from the obsession with older men, Claire was a good girl. Smart, funny, good at school, lots of friends. She was well-rounded with a bright future ahead of her... unless this behavior continued.

The lying, the cheating, the hiding. It was awful, and way too heavy for an eighteen-year-old to try and juggle. Kate remembered back to when she was eighteen—she'd been a mess of hormones and emotions, way too immature to handle something as complicated as an affair with a married man. She didn't know how Claire had the patience for it, or the mental capacity.

"I'm going to go and have a nap," Kate said slowly, rising from the stool at the breakfast bar to make her way over to Claire.

When she was standing over her daughter, she planted a kiss on the top of her head.

Oh, my baby, Kate thought. *When did everything get so messed up?*

Author's Note: for a big thick, full-length novel about Claire and her affair with the married man, read my book *Demanding Husband*.

Chapter Three

Need so much more

As SHE CLIMBED THE stairs to her bedroom, Kate tried not to think about all the times she'd caught Claire cozying up to older men. It had been persistent, pervasive, almost extreme. Every man that Kate brought into the house, Claire showed an interest in.

It always started innocently enough but, within a short space of time, Claire had always made her wants perfectly clear. Some men had run for the hills as soon as she tried to touch them inappropriately which, no doubt, only made her obsession worse.

But some men allowed her to continue, whether it was through desire or shock, and that wasn't great either. The number of times Kate had screamed at her daughter—and her tutors—it was ludicrous. No matter what she did or how she tried to talk her daughter down, the behavior still continued.

Stop, Kate thought. *Stop thinking about this. It's not going to help.*

It wasn't going to help. Thinking about Claire's weird fantasies about older men wasn't going to help anything. It was only going to make her angrier. She just focused on her feet hitting against the carpeted stairs, thudding gently as she made her way to the top.

The large, open hallway was bright with sunlight. All of the doors were open, allowing light to stream out of every room, making the whole upstairs feel more open than it actually was.

On the left, over the entrance to the house, was Kate's home gym. Next to it was her office. Wedged between the office and the guest bedroom was the guest bathroom. Then it was Kate's bedroom, then Claire's right in front of the stairs.

Kate went into her bedroom and closed the door behind her, no doubt dimming the light in the hallway a little. She didn't care. Straight ahead of her, against the longest wall in the room, was her huge bed. It was way too much space for just one person, but that was the way she liked it. After all, wasn't that one of the perks of being single—all that extra bed space?

Built into the wall to her right was a closet with mirrored sliding doors hiding the clothes. She looked at herself as she passed the mirror, heading straight for the bed.

It was clear that she'd been crying. Her face was blotchy and her eyes were red. It was nice of Claire not to say anything about it, really. Dark bags were hanging beneath her eyes, making her look ten years older than she actually was.

Kate stretched out on her bed and considered taking a nap. Her body was exhausted and aching, as was her mind. But she didn't want to sleep. There was a part of her, deep inside, that felt wholly unsatisfied with the day.

Everything was coming down hard on her shoulders, making everything feel bleak and cold. She knew there was only one thing she could do to make sure she enjoyed a peaceful, dreamless sleep.

Kate rolled off the edge of her bed and crouched down, her hands extended out beneath the bed, searching for the familiar plastic surface. It was somewhere under there, she just had to find it.

When her fingers connected with the cold plastic, Kate's hands clamped down and dragged the box out. She heaved as hard as she could, yanking until she fell back onto her ass.

The box was filled to the very brim. Kate let her hands drift over the lid, feeling the lumps and bumps where the plastic was stretched over the contents. The lid was lifting in some areas. She had too many things in there.

Her huge box was in desperate need of a clean-out, but Kate couldn't bring herself to part with anything in there. Everything had its use, perfect for a certain time, mood, and place.

Kate let her hands fall down to the sides and lifted up the plastic locks. The lid instantly popped off, revealing a brightly colored mess of shapes and sizes in the box.

Her eyes bulged and her teeth sank into her bottom lip as she stared into the box. There were so many silicone cocks in front of her, so many that it was almost impossible for her to choose.

Kate put the lid down on the floor and began rummaging through the box. Just touching the dildos made blood rush down to the spot between her legs. She could feel her pussy tighten in her underwear, starting to pulse and engorge.

Most of them were anatomically correct, with nuts at the base and veins popping out of the sides, but not all of them had the same toughness. Some were rock hard, rigid, that wouldn't give way if you mounted it on the bed. Others were softer, easier to twist from side to side to reach unexplored areas.

All of them were huge, though. Kate knew what she liked and it wasn't a tiny cock. She liked her cocks huge, wide, and big enough to fill her insides completely. To her, there was no better sensation.

Today was no exception. She tossed aside her small dildos and vibrators, wanting to find something monster to fill her hole. She knew exactly the one, too... The perfect cock to fit her terrible mood.

Years ago, one of her girlfriends had persuaded her to go to a porn convention. At first, Kate had thought it was a skeezy, disgusting place. Only sluts and porn addicts went there, their cocks in hand ready to meet their favorite star. It hadn't taken her long to warm up to the place, though.

People were so open with their sexuality. It was out there for the whole world to see. There was no shame, no hiding. Kate had felt a freedom she hadn't ever felt before.

That was where she'd brought her first dildo. It had been a huge one, too huge for her back then, and she'd mostly bought it as a joke. A gag gift for herself to remind her that she could still have fun even though her husband had abandoned her.

For a couple of years, that dildo had stayed hidden in her bedroom, without so much as a stroke or a touch. Kate could see the error of her ways now, of course. When she was having a bad day, it was that cock she always went back to.

When she finally found it, buried at the bottom, she wrenched it out of the box and held it up in front of her. It was a dark purple, a royal color, huge and covered in veins. The head was massive, wobbling as she held it up in her weak arms.

As she stared at the cock she'd come to love, she couldn't help but remember how awful she'd been at the convention. How shy, how giggly, how pathetic. Kate knew that she'd evolved into the perfect specimen now. She was wild, fierce, and completely unmatched. This was her true form, how she always wanted to be.

Kate lowered the cock as she let her hands stroke up and down the shaft. A smile crept onto her lips as she remembered how she used to be. Such a prude, such a good girl, so innocent and sweet. It was stupid and it made Kate cringe just to think about it.

Now wasn't a time for thinking, though. Now was a time for pleasing. Kate held the fake cock in her hand as she stood up. Both of her knees cracked beneath her, one after the other. She tried to ignore the feeling as she made her way to the bed, still staring at the huge cock she was about to put inside of her.

It was all she could focus on, swaying through the air as she climbed onto her bed. Her laptop was tucked inside her bedside table, along with tubes of lube and a box of tissues. Kate brought the whole lot out before stripping off her clothes.

She didn't even bother getting under the covers. She was too hot, too excited. The only thing she wanted was to fuck herself hard, to make herself cum until she could barely breathe.

Kate opened her laptop and found her way to her favorite porn site. Most of the videos weren't to her liking—there was one specific theme that she always liked to enjoy: dominatrix.

She wasn't sure how this obsession had started. It was a little while after she'd brought her first dildo. Bored of masturbating in a dark room, she decided to see what all the fuss was about. She was intrigued, even though most of the videos didn't do anything for her.

Who wanted to see women deep-throating men's cocks? Not her, that was for sure. She had stumbled upon her preferred porn just out of sheer curiosity. An accidental click, a little skipping-forward, and she had seen women do unspeakable things to willing men.

It had turned her on more than anything else in her life. The first orgasm she'd had while watching it was intense, better than anything any man had given her, and from then on she was hooked.

The best part for Kate was imagining herself doing those things to men. Treading on them with high-heeled shoes, whipping them with leather and rods, tying them up in compromising positions, and being able to do whatever she wanted to their fragile, delicate bodies.

It didn't take long for her to find a video that whetted her appetite. A large-breasted blonde woman, scantily clad in pleather, cracked her whip against the floor. Her platform shoes were impossibly high with daggers for heels. A waxed and sweating man was positioned on the floor, his chest heaving as he looked up to his master…

That was all Kate needed to see. Her underwear was soaked through with her arousal, her whole body thumping in time with her heart. She grabbed hold of her monster dildo and gently smoothed on a little bit of water-based lube. She knew that she didn't need it, but she wanted to be safe rather than sorry.

As soon as she pressed the silicone head to her lower lips, she gasped. It was cool and soft against her, caressing her skin as she moved her hips up and down, getting her juices all over the head.

Her legs were parted, her knees up high, and between her legs she could see the screen. The woman was whipping the floor near the man's body, walking around as she shouted something down to him.

Kate couldn't hear what the woman was saying—this laptop was perpetually mute for Claire's sake—but she didn't care. Their words were meaningless. What mattered was the acts, what they were doing to one another.

Gently, she eased the dildo inside of herself. She gasped and moaned quietly, keeping her voice low so her daughter didn't hear. It didn't take long for her hips to start bucking, grinding on the cock that was slowly entering her.

Kate didn't like taking it so slow. She was impatient, she wanted it all and she wanted it now, but she had to take it slow. It was too big not to. Ever so slowly, she felt herself enveloping the cock. The ridges and bumps of the fake veins gave it a beautiful ribbed feeling, sending shivers up and down her spine.

The muscles in her pussy were already tight, the same with the muscles in her stomach and legs. She was so close to cumming already, but she didn't want to blow her load just yet. She wanted to savor this moment, to enjoy it as much as she could.

She kept moving the cock in and out, slowly easing it deeper and deeper, as sweat started to soak her forehead. Her eyes never left the screen, watching as the women berated the man. Without thinking, she moved her right hand to her clitoris.

Her fingers slipped down between her lips momentarily, before moving back up, bringing lube and her juices along. She rubbed her fingers around her clit in circles, trying to intensify the feeling growing inside her.

It was like a fireball was embedded into her pelvis, just waiting to be released. All of her muscles were tense and ready to release, even if she wasn't.

Kate's fingers moved faster and faster as her eyes focused on the screen, watching the woman take her first tentative steps onto the man's back. His skin instantly turned white under the pressure, the stick-thin stiletto heels digging deep into his flesh.

Her teeth gritted together as her fingers moved faster, going around and around as her whole body turned hot to the touch. She could feel it coming, building, growing ever stronger as she edged herself to orgasm.

And then it rolled over her. Her whole pussy clenched and released in a sweet, glorious rhythm. Trembles rushed through her whole body as her fingers slowed. She couldn't stop her stomach from crunching, drawing her whole torso forwards as all of the tension left her body.

It only lasted a second, but it was so very worth it. Kate relaxed back on the bed, panting and sweating, as she stared up to the ceiling.

Not enough, Kate thought as she tried to regain control of her lungs. *Not long enough at all.*

It didn't matter, though. She had the rest of the night to please herself. This was only the beginning.

Chapter Four

Keep it together

As soon as Kate's eyes peeled open, a horrible, heavy feeling pressed against her body. The covers were warm and soft against her skin but it wasn't enough to soothe her. She pulled the covers high over her head and buried herself in the darkness, hoping that the day would melt away.

It didn't. The day kept pressing on. Downstairs, Claire was banging around in the kitchen as she got herself ready for school. Kate was glad she was old enough to take care of herself these days. She couldn't imagine pulling herself out of bed for a needy, young child today.

The worst part of it all was that the day wasn't going to go anywhere. Kate had nothing but time on her hands now. The day wasn't going to vanish by burying herself in her work. She didn't have any work. It had been taken away from her.

The only things she could do all day were to lie on her back and stare at the ceiling. How much fun was that, honestly? She couldn't pleasure herself anymore. She'd already rammed herself raw. There was no way she was going to be able to go down there again. She was going to make herself chafe otherwise.

Kate rolled onto her side and huffed heavily, wondering what she was going to do with her day. Sit around? Watch bad TV? Eat her body weight in chocolate and bread?

It all sounded so foreign to her. Ever since her ex-husband had left her, she'd morphed into a strong, powerful woman that didn't let anything get in her way. This whole not-being-allowed-to-work thing felt an awful lot like bullcrap to her.

Kate threw back the covers and stared around at her white room. She'd demanded that everything be white. The furniture, the walls, the ceiling, the carpet. Now that she saw it in the cold light of day, she knew that it was too sterile. What had she been thinking?

I was thinking that I never spent serious time in here, Kate thought. *Why would I want this room to have character if I never spent time in it? I just wanted it to look clean.*

The last time Kate had spent this much time in her bedroom was a couple of years ago when she got the flu. Even then she didn't care what the room looked like. She just wanted out. But now she had time to sit and think about her choices. And the only thing she could think was that this choice was wrong.

Kate wasn't the type of woman to sit around and mope. She knew she had to get up and start her day, even if she had nothing planned. She pulled her laptop out of her bedside table and opened it up quickly. Once her history was cleared, she closed the lid and went to her closet.

She didn't bother to search for something cute. When her hands found the softest, comfiest clothes she had, she shuffled her body into them and stuffed her laptop beneath her arm.

Claire was still in the kitchen, sorting out her breakfast and lunch for the day. Kate didn't feel like talking to anyone but she knew she had to step up and be a good mother. She'd been absent for a lot of Claire's life—it was the least she could do.

"Good morning," Kate said dully as she came into the kitchen.

Claire looked over her shoulder as she reached into the cupboards above her. "Hey, mom," she said. "How you doin'?"

"Fine," Kate sighed.

She set the laptop on the breakfast bar and sat in front of it, her tired eyes feeling droopy as she opened the computer up.

"How's school?" Kate asked, sounding completely uninterested, even to herself.

"Fine," Claire said, pausing for a second. "Are you going to tell me the truth?"

She placed her bowl on the marble countertop between them and stared at Kate's face. There was no bluffing Claire. She had this skill—she could see past anyone's charades, even if she'd just met them. Kate wanted to know where her daughter had picked up this incredible ability but she'd never been able to figure out how she had come to acquire it. Kate resigned herself to the fact that her daughter was just a genius and she'd never have that level of intelligence.

"Work stuff," Kate sighed. "It's nothing."

She tried to smile but it failed. It didn't reach her eyes. Hell, it didn't even reach her cheeks. The edges of her lips curled upwards awkwardly.

"Mom," Claire sighed. "Are you still whining about that?"

Kate stared at her daughter, shocked.

"Most people would kill for some time off," Claire said. "Why don't you stop moping and start enjoying yourself?"

Kate looked down at her laptop in front of her, the cursor hovering over her email client. She knew Claire was right. Totally and completely right. But that didn't make it any easier for Kate. She needed to work. It was a part of her personality, a vital part of her identity. Without her job... who was she?

No, Kate thought quickly. *Don't pull at that thread. Distract yourself.*

Kate smiled again, this time making it a little more convincing. "You're right," she said. "I'm too in my head. I need to enjoy this time while I have it."

"Right," Claire smiled. "And, while you're enjoying your time, you should totally bring me with you."

Kate eyed her daughter carefully. Now she understood why she cared so much. It wasn't that she was worried about her stressed-out mother. Oh, no. Her cheeky teenage mind was looking for a way to get a free vacation during the school year.

"I don't think so," Kate chuckled. "I think you need to concentrate on your studies."

"Oh, come on," Claire moaned, grinning from ear to ear. "We could both use a vacation. Somewhere hot. Somewhere with plenty of sunshine."

Kate could have rolled her eyes into the back of her head. It was so obvious now. So clear what her daughter so desperately craved.

"Nope," Kate smiled. "But, now that you mention it, I might go somewhere warm without you."

Claire's face dropped in an instant. "You wouldn't *dare*."

"You put the idea there," Kate said.

Her hands grabbed either side of her laptop and pulled it closer to her. With her finger on the trackpad, she moved her cursor from her emails to her browser. A quick double click and everything was loading.

Kate knew exactly where she wanted to go—South America. Somewhere cheap, somewhere fancy, and somewhere warm. Claire was smarter than she looked. Somehow she knew exactly what it was that Kate was craving.

"So," Claire said, the cheeky tone back in her voice, "does this mean that I get to stay home alone while you're gone?"

"Hm," Kate thought. "I don't know. Maybe I'll hire a sitter for three weeks to watch you."

Claire only stared at her mother, her eyes icy cold. "I can't believe you would even *think* of doing that to me," she snapped. "I'm *eighteen,* not eight."

"It was a joke," Kate said as she began her search. "Calm down... or I *will* hire a sitter."

That didn't help Claire's little tantrum. She poured out a bowl of cereal in silence. It was clear she was fuming. Kate didn't even have to look up to know it. She could feel Claire radiating hate through the air.

Kate tried to ignore it as best as she could. After all, she'd been a moody teenager once. With all those hormones rushing through the body, it was hard to keep a cool head. She remembered how it had been, even if the memory was distant and faded.

It didn't take Claire long to finish off her breakfast and storm off upstairs. Once her back was turned, Kate couldn't help but break out into a smile. All teenagers were so melodramatic and hers wasn't much better. Of course, life was difficult, but it wasn't *that* difficult.

Kate knew that in a couple of years, Claire would get over this spell and she'd be back to a normal human being. For now, she'd just have to grin and bear her daughter's mood swings. Trying to ignore the stomping feet above her, Kate went back to looking at her laptop.

All she wanted was a cheap getaway, something to burn the time she was now faced with. She scrolled through a couple of websites, looking at all the destination packages they offered. Kate couldn't be bothered booking everything herself—she just wanted to hand over a lump sum of money to a company and have them take care of all the details.

A couple of the places looked fantastic. Big, beautiful rooms in gleaming hotels with their own gyms, dozens of swimming pools, spas... The list was endless. Kate was lapping up all of the information, imagining herself spread out on a lounger, soaking up the hot sun.

A shiver ran down her spine then. It was perfect. She needed somewhere warm—hot, even—so she could come back home with a beautiful tan to make her even more confident.

When Kate saw a beautiful beachfront hotel in Argentina, she was instantly sold. The sand on the beach was light and warm, the sea was a crystal blue that matched the sky, and the straw umbrellas looked quaint in the best possible way. In the distance of the pictures, she could see women sunning themselves with large shades and huge brimmed hats.

Kate knew that she wanted to be one of those women. She wanted to be on that beach, soaking up the sun with every inch of her body. Nothing could have stopped her from booking the vacation. She was sold. She was going. There was nothing to think about.

After she'd paid for the vacation, a horrifying thought struck her. Claire was going to use this chance to further her affair with the married man. That was the only downside to all of this. Kate leaned back in her seat as she waited for her confirmation email, thinking about what this could mean for Claire.

Kate worried about her. There was no way this wasn't going to end in trouble... but what kind of trouble?

Claire wasn't going to get accidentally pregnant. Kate was *sure* of that. As soon as Claire had mentioned that she was sexually active, Kate had taken her to the doctor and gotten her an implant. No forgetting to take pills, no entrapping the man for eighteen years worth of child support.

The only other trouble it could mean is that Claire breaks up their marriage. Or, even less likely, that her married man could leave his wife and try to be with Claire.

A knot formed in Kate's stomach as she thought about a middle-aged man making moves on her daughter. There was nothing she could do short of contacting the police, and that would ruin her relationship with Claire and it would ruin the man's life. Sure, it was wrong of him to pursue Claire, but she was involved in this as well. She was eighteen. Just scarcely legal.

Kate dragged her laptop a little bit closer to the edge of the breakfast bar. Within a second she'd opened a new tab and gone straight to Claire's chosen social media page. She looked at the blue outlines around the page as she stalked her daughter.

Of course, nothing was public. Her profile looked like the normal teenage feed. Pictures of her and her friends, far too many pictures of herself, and even more angsty posts about how everything sucks.

Kate looked through Claire's friend list, trying to find his familiar face. She'd known his name for a long time but somehow she always managed to forget it, even though he was some huge deal in the architect world.

There he was. Vince Bugatti. Kate clicked on his face, bringing up his profile. In his picture, it was easy to see his dark hair and beard. The beginnings of wrinkles around his eyes and the corners of his mouth were deep, making him look more dignified than he probably was. His clothes exuded wealth, a crisp suit paired with a crisp, linen, open-collared shirt.

Vince was being caressed by his wife. Tight dress, high heels, the lady could have easily been a model in her younger days. And her daughter was getting between that, ruining what could be a happy marriage.

She wasn't just blaming Claire, though. Vince was deserving of the blame as well. He made vows before his friends and family to love and cherish his wife. Kate knew that cheating wasn't included in that. She didn't know how Vince could even stomach sleeping with her? It was disgusting.

There was no point in thinking about it and there was definitely no point in stalking their social media. It was all fake. People only uploaded the best parts of their life. They weren't going to air their dirty laundry to the world. After all, wasn't that exactly what Kate was guilty of? She wasn't posting on social media about having to take a month off work.

Besides, there wasn't much Kate could do to fix all of this. Anything she did to get Vince in trouble would literally ruin his life and his wife's as well. Claire would likely never speak to her again, either.

It was best if she just let it play out however it was going to play out. Claire was going off to college in less than six months. Either they'd have to go long distance, or Claire would have to commute back and forth to keep seeing him.

Their relationship—if Kate could even call it that—wouldn't last forever. Soon it would fizzle out and there would be nothing left but bad memories and regret. Sure, Claire didn't see that now, but she would when she was older. Then Kate could shrug and say: *I told you so.*

A gentle pinging sound emanated from her laptop. A small notice in the bottom left corner of her screen told her that the confirmation email had come through. That was it. She was going on vacation. As easy as that.

Thundering footsteps came down the stairs as Claire rushed toward the front door. Kate looked through their open-plan home and saw Claire's dark red bag slung over one shoulder. She rushed to the front door, slipped on her sneakers, and yanked down hard on the handle.

"See ya later, Mom!" she called, looking over her shoulder as she rushed out the door.

Kate called out goodbye after her, suddenly feeling tired. Watching her daughter sprint around like that was exhausting. How did Vince keep up with her? She was a young, vibrant woman, being held back by an old man. Surely he couldn't feel young with her. Even Kate felt old in Claire's energetic presence and she wasn't anywhere near Vince's age.

Kate didn't want to think about it anymore. She had some packing to do. Her flight was in two days. That was plenty of time to get everything together, to prepare Claire, and to get the hell out of there.

Chapter Five

All eyes on you

THE HEAT WAS THE first thing to hit Kate. It was like walking onto the freeway and having an eighteen-wheeler run her down. The sweltering temperature was unimaginable, as was the humidity. Who in their right mind could live like this?

As soon as Kate had stepped off the plane, she had felt her body start to melt. And that was at nine at night, local time. It was awful, sitting on a crowded sweaty bus as she was shuttled to her hotel. She knew she should have splurged for a taxi, but she hadn't thought that far ahead. Clearly.

The clothes she'd worn onto the plane were too tight, too clingy, too *hot*. Kate couldn't handle it. The whole night, all she could think about was how she'd made a terrible mistake. Even in the air-conditioned hotel room, she could barely stand breathing in the thick, hot air.

When the sun rose in front of her balcony, the sun filtering through her open curtains, Kate's eyes opened and she took in a deep breath. Somehow, the air had cleared. All of the muggy air had been wiped away, replaced by a warm breeze and fresh, breathable air. Kate stepped out onto the balcony, her silk nightgown hanging down in the middle of her thighs, and felt the whole world come into view.

She was on the upper levels of the hotel, looking down at the rest of the world around her. Below her, she could see the hotel pool along with the guests sunning themselves in the early morning rays. People were walking around everywhere with large hats and purses. Kate could almost hear the sounds of their sandals crashing against the soles of their feet.

The delicate smell of salt was in the air, wafting into her hair. Kate inhaled deeply, feeling the scent invigorate her. This was exactly what she needed. The previous night had been hellish, but today had almost entirely made up for it. How could she have thought this was a bad idea? Soaking up the sun in South America was *never* bad.

Kate went back inside her hotel room to get dressed. She would have to choose something loose-fitting to keep herself cool. She chose a linen shirt and a flowing cotton skirt, something pleasant to go down and eat breakfast in. After that, she knew she would shed her clothes to reveal her bikini beneath. Nothing was going to stop her from going down to that beach and sinking her toes into the sand.

The hotel lobby was more beautiful than she'd remembered. It had been covered in a cloud of darkness when she'd arrived the previous night. But now it gleamed in the daylight, sparkling from top to bottom. The marble floors were immaculate. The bars and desks were sleek and modern, made of glass and white painted wood. Chairs and glass tables were scattered around, unused.

The dining area was much of the same. It was buffet-style, with hundreds of tables covered in white cloth. Kate perused the buffet before choosing a simple fruit salad to start her day. It wasn't something she'd usually choose at home, what with it being filled with sugar, but she figured that it was time to splurge. After all, she was on vacation.

Little paper containers were at the end of the buffet, where you could take leftovers with you for the rest of the day. Kate did just that, packing herself a small roll of bread, some fruit, and even a couple of muffins.

Now that she had lunch sorted, she was free to follow her heart to the beach. That was where she really wanted to be. That had been the biggest selling factor in this hotel. With her food in her purse, she made her way out of the dining area and into a small patio.

It was covered in shining tiles with loungers and tables and chairs. A couple of bars were dotted around the place with dark-skinned men in white shirts serving elegant-looking drinks. Kate tried to keep her eyes straight ahead of her, aimed right at the beach.

Nothing was going to distract her. Not the splashes and gleeful giggles coming from the pool to her right, nor the shaking sounds of cocktails to her left. The only thing she needed was the beach.

The warm yellow sands were ahead of her, shining so brightly beneath the hot sun. Only a couple more feet and she'd be there, in the sand, with the sun blaring down from above. She could feel her heart racing in her chest as she approached.

People were everywhere. Tall men in shorts and small, skinny women in bathing suits. All of them had large smiles on their faces, their white teeth laughing out at the world.

Kate felt her foot sink into the ground, her skin suddenly enveloped by something silky and warm. When she glanced down, she saw that her foot was being swallowed by the sand. A huge smile came onto her lips, natural and free, as she felt the warmth of the sand wrapping around her skin.

Just the feeling of it sent tingles shooting up her legs. She pulled her foot from the sand and began to walk, feeling her body sinking as she took each step. A happy laugh came out of her mouth, a sweet giggling sound, as she tried to get to a free lounger.

She didn't care that she looked like an idiot, or that she was kicking up sand to her waist, or that people were staring. None of that mattered. The only thing that mattered was that she was here. She was enjoying herself.

Kate found a lounger and sat down in it, laughing to herself as she thought about how crazy life was. Only days ago, her boss had told her to take time off work. At the time, she'd thought it was the end of her career. Now she didn't seem to care. When she thought about it, it didn't weigh heavy on her heart. If anything, she felt lighter now.

It wasn't clear to her how getting away from her home and her family could make her feel so much better but she wasn't going to ignore it.

Kate relaxed onto the lounger and felt the sun beat down on her clothed body. For now, she was comfortable enough in her clothes, but soon she would get too hot and that's when she'd reveal her bikini-clad body to the world.

"Miss," a thickly accented voice said. "Can I get you something to drink?"

Confused, Kate looked around to try and see where the voice was coming from. She finally found his face. He was standing by the head of her lounger, his hands clasped behind his back. Kate craned her neck back to see him properly and smiled widely.

"Oh, thank you," Kate started, "but how much will it cost?"

"It is free," the man said, bowing slightly. "The hotel is all-inclusive."

Then he paused, frowning a little, and edged closer to her.

"You are staying at the Felicity Hotel, aren't you?"

Kate lifted her wrist to show him her bright purple wristband, given to her at the courtesy of the hotel's front desk when she checked in. She'd been told the wristband would give her access to all their amenities, inside and out.

"Wonderful," he said cheerily. "So, can I get you something?"

"I'll have a Sex on the Beach," Kate said.

It was the first drink that came to her mind. As soon as the words came out of her mouth, she regretted them. The man's pleasant smile faltered as he stared at her. Kate wasn't going to let her embarrassment show, though. She just smiled at the man and nodded.

He scurried off to arrange her the drink while she ruminated on everything that poor man was probably thinking. Kate knew that his mind probably went to the most obvious place—that he was being hit on.

That wasn't what she'd meant at all, though. She was just excited to be here, at the beach, leaving all of her worries back home. Clearly, not all of her worries were gone. She was still able to feel shame, and the heat was slowly rising up into her cheeks.

Kate was determined not to blush. She fanned herself, pretending to be hot from the sun when she heard a light chuckle coming from a couple of loungers away.

She sat up in her chair and looked at the man to her left. He had tanned skin, dark hair, and a thick layer of stubble along his jaw and cheeks. His beautifully straight teeth were poking out from his smiling lips as he chuckled.

Kate didn't want to come out and ask him what his problem was, but she was half-tempted. The man just kept on chuckling as he flicked through his glossy magazine.

"Are you laughing at me?" Kate asked, leaning forward with her elbows digging into her knees.

The man looked over at her. That was when she got the first good look at his face. He was young, young enough to be her son, with the most stunning blue eyes she'd ever seen. They were embedded into his face, surrounded by the silky tanned skin and dark hair atop his head.

If he weren't so young, Kate would have immediately dug her claws into him. She couldn't, though. She was far, far too old.

"Not at you," he said, his voice purring as he spoke. "With you."

Kate squinted at him. "I'm not laughing."

She wasn't going to let him off just because he was cute. How often had that worked for him? How often had he been able to be rude and degrading to women, only to have them pool pathetically at his feet? Not Kate. She could separate her brain from her pussy.

"You will be," the man said. "Don't worry."

Kate couldn't quite work out where his accent was from. She knew it was European, that much was obvious, but she didn't know which one. Italian? Spanish? Christ, even French? She couldn't be sure. She'd never been to any of those countries. She'd never really listened to the language or heard them speak English, so she wasn't going to be able to guess.

"What kind of accent is that, anyway?" She asked, leaning back into her lounger.

The man let the magazine fall down to his lap. "Are you asking me where I'm from?"

"Sure," Kate said, raising her arms above her head to tuck them behind the lounger.

"I'm from Italy," he said, his voice rolling all of the syllables he spoke. "I don't need to ask where you're from."

Kate let her head fall to the left, her eyes staring into his beautiful face. "No?" She asked, smiling. "And why is that?"

"Your accent," he said. "So very clearly American."

He paused, picked up his magazine, and began to pretend to read.

"That," he added, "and your sheer arrogance."

Kate couldn't stop the scoff from bursting out of her mouth. It was followed by a round of laughter. There was no stopping it. The last time a man spoke to her like that, she'd fired him.

"See?" He asked, looking over at her. "I told you you'd be laughing."

Kate nodded slowly, letting her laughs gently ease off. "You got me," she said.

There was no other way to put it—this guy was cocky. She usually didn't like cocky guys but this one had her interested. Was there a reason he was so confident? Was he well endowed? Or did he just think he was better than everyone else?

She took a little sip of her Sex on the Beach. The peach and orange taste slipped over her tongue and down her throat, cooling her off instantly.

Without her asking him, he got up off his lounger and sat down on the one next to hers. Kate eyed him suspiciously as he sat down beside her. She rolled her shoulders as she leaned into her lounger, a little annoyed that he'd presumed she wanted him closer.

He sat on the edge of the lounger, staring at her with his elbows buried into his knees. Kate didn't want to encourage his behavior, so she tried to ignore him as she sipped at her drink.

"How about I take you out for dinner?" He asked, raising his eyebrows as he spoke.

"Dinner?" Kate asked, incredulous. "I don't even know your name."

The man held out his hand. "Gerard," he said, rolling the R's in his name. "And you are?"

Kate shook his hand gently, slowly. "Kate."

"A beautiful name for a beautiful woman," he said, his voice so silky it grated against Kate's nerves.

"You're not as smooth as you think you are," Kate said, trying to pick at his confidence.

No man was as smooth as Gerard was. Not naturally, at least. It had to be an act or at least an extremely good day. She wanted to dig a little beneath the surface to see what was lurking behind the façade.

"Come on," he said. "What will it hurt to spend an evening with me?"

Kate raised her eyebrows and looked at him expectantly. "I don't know you," she said. "You could be a murderer. Or a psychopath. Or something."

"Fine," he sighed. "Dinner in the hotel, then. Safe with plenty of eyes on us."

Kate tried not to smirk. "You are persistent," she said slowly.

She set her drink on the small glass table beside her and looked purposefully into his eyes. Christ, if she wasn't so jaded, those eyes might have melted her down to her very core. It wasn't like Kate was going to catch feelings and run away with this guy. She knew herself better than that.

He was cute, anyway. And he was clearly doing well for himself—a European in South America, which wasn't a cheap journey. The idea that he would come all this way to commit murder was kind of ridiculous. It would have been wiser to go to another country closer to home.

But she wasn't going to let him know about that thought. It was best to keep some distance between them. If she didn't, he'd only get cockier. That wasn't what Kate wanted. If anything, she wanted to break him. It would take some work, but she knew she'd be able to do it.

"Fine," she sighed. "Dinner. In the hotel."

"Excellent," he said. "How does eight sound?"

Kate shrugged. "Sounds fine," she said. "I'll see you there."

Right now, she wanted him to go away. This was the first day she'd spent on her vacation and she wanted to spend it alone, not playing with some boy who barely knew how to please a woman.

Kate felt a sigh of relief rush out of her nose as Gerard collected his belongings and left the beach. She was surprised he was leaving instead of hanging around to enjoy the sunshine, but she didn't really care. It was none of her business. She was here to enjoy herself and that's exactly what she was going to do.

No boy was going to distract her from that... unless she could have her own kind of fun with him.

Chapter Six

Woman on top

THAT NIGHT, KATE FOUND herself at dinner with Gerard. She had chosen a table in the center of the dining room, surrounded by staff and guests alike. There was no way Gerard would be able to do anything to her, but she wasn't really concerned about that.

The hotel staff were busy going around the tables, filling up the water and wine glasses. Most of the food was served on a buffet but there was a small menu of main courses and desserts that were made to order.

Kate didn't want any of that—she'd helped herself to a salad at the buffet and kept filling up on wine. She had to, really. Being on a date with such a young guy wasn't an easy thing to stomach.

Over the dinner, she'd learned that he was an eye-watering age of twenty-one years old. He could only just about drink. Kate knew she had no business being with him on this date, leading him on, but he was clearly interested.

Kate watched as he reached across the table and took her hand in his.

"You are the most beautiful woman I've ever seen," he said, whispering so quietly that Kate strained to hear him. "Just stunning. Perfection."

Kate wanted to roll her eyes and pat his hand condescendingly. "Oh, honey," she sighed. "You're young. You don't know what beauty really is."

He frowned at her deeply. "What do you mean?"

"You're young," Kate said, removing her hand from beneath his. "You just don't know the true meaning of beauty yet."

Gerard looked confused for a moment. "A beautiful face," he said slowly. "That's the meaning of beauty, no?"

Kate nodded as she sipped at her red wine. She wasn't going to argue with him. She worked hard to look nice, sure, but *her* beauty wasn't skin-deep.

As people aged, it became clear that looks weren't everything. Over the years, beauty fades, and what was left was what was inside. If you were a bad person on the inside, you weren't beautiful, no matter how great you looked.

There was no point talking to him about all of this. He was a young, hormone-fueled boy who had almost no life experience. Hell, he was still in college, here taking a quick break between exams.

"You said you're in college?" Kate asked, trying to distract him. "What are you studying?"

"English," Gerard said, his voice sultry and quiet. "I love reading old, romantic stories from England's history."

Kate felt the cynicism rising inside of her. "Like Romeo and Juliet?" She asked. "Those kinds of stories?"

"Yes," Gerard whispered excitedly. "Yes, Shakespeare is one of my favorites. I love his works. We study his plays at school all the time."

"Of course," Kate nodded, trying to sound upbeat.

She found it hard, though. What was romantic about the two leads dying in the end? That wasn't something she thought people should aspire to.

"And what else do you like to read?" She asked. "Anything modern?"

"No," Gerard shook his head. "Some poetry, but nothing modern really. It's all so... trashy."

Trashy, Kate thought. *Why is he interested in me?*

Kate had been called trashy so many times in her life. Sleeping with men whenever she liked, displaying her body in any way she pleased, and staying a single mother instead of getting remarried. All of those things made her somewhat trashy back home.

He's European, Kate reminded herself. *They have different definitions of family, or what's trashy.*

"What do you like to do for fun?" Kate asked.

She set her wine back on the table between them, and watched as Gerard smiled at the change of conversation. Then he leaned in closer to her, his eyes sparkling.

"Making love," he said. "Looking at the stars. Reading, writing, but mostly poetry."

Poetry again, Kate thought. *Christ, he really believes in this stuff.*

She didn't want to shit all over his ideals so she politely nodded and smiled. Just being in his presence made her feel so broken. Life hadn't given her the best of times and she had accepted that, but being around someone so green and eager made her heart sting.

She hated feeling sorry for herself, so she pushed her thoughts aside and tried to ignore her pangs of jealousy.

"What about you?" Gerard asked. "What do you like to do?"

Kate wasn't going to hide any aspect of herself, no matter how much it might scare him. She made herself comfortable in her chair before speaking.

"Well, I'm a Director of Product Development for an electronics company," she said slowly, making sure Gerard understood what she was saying. "I don't have a lot of free time but I do enjoy my job."

Gerard frowned. "So you just work?" He asked, sounding sad.

"A lot of the time," Kate said. "I also have a daughter at home, so she takes up a lot of my time as well."

Gerard only frowned deeper. "A husband, too?"

Kate shook her head. She wasn't going to open her lips on that subject. To her surprise, there was no judgment in his eyes. He just nodded, accepted what she said, and moved on to his next question.

"How old is your daughter?" Gerard asked.

"Old enough to be left alone on her own for a couple of weeks," Kate said, smiling.

As much as she didn't want to hide parts of her life from him, she knew that admitting that she had an eighteen-year-old daughter was going to spook him.

Kate thought Gerard was impossibly cute and she knew where she wanted this evening to lead to: steamy, hot sex in her hotel room.

"You must have been very young," he said smoothly. "So, you work and come home, and that's it?"

Kate smiled. "I'm here now," she said. "So no, I suppose not."

"How did such a busy woman like yourself manage to get time off work?" Gerard asked. "Isn't the company going to fall apart without you?"

Kate laughed, a little louder this time, and reached for her wine in reflex. She was using it as a shield to protect herself.

"Oh, it might," she said, before taking a big sip from her glass. "But I'm sure I'll be able to fix everything when I get back."

"A capable woman," he said slowly.

Then he leaned back in his chair, letting his eyes drift over Kate's body. It was clear he was appreciating her, inside and out.

Kate wasn't going to tell him off for looking. She wanted him to whet his appetite because she knew where this night was heading, even if he didn't. Being open and honest about what she wanted was the only way she was going to be able to get what she needed from him.

"So, are there any men back home?" Gerard asked. "Any angry boyfriends that might come after me for taking you to dinner?"

Kate smiled. "You're hardly taking me anywhere," she said. "This hotel is all-inclusive."

Gerard didn't accept her deflecting his question. He just stared at her, his bright blue eyes boring into hers.

They'd only been on their date for thirty minutes or so. She wasn't ready to lay her cards on the table so early, but Gerard was forcing her hand.

"Look," she sighed, leaning forward a little. "I'm not looking for a relationship. Here, or back home. My life is full enough as it is. I don't need a man to complete me. What I do want, however, is a quick vacation fling that I'll be able to remember for years to come. Do you understand?"

She looked deeply into Gerard's eyes and watched as the recognition flickered through them. Her words sank into his mind, taking root there as his imagination, no doubt, ran wild.

"A quick fling," Gerard said, smirking. "That is something I can be comfortable with."

Kate raised her eyebrows. "Are you sure?" She asked. "I'm not going to change my mind and get all emotional just because we fucked one night."

Gerard's eyes widened at the last word. He ripped his eyes from hers and glanced around the dining hall. Luckily, no one was nearby. No one was listening to their conversation. When Gerard brought his eyes back to Kate, there was a glint in them.

"So, what are we doing here?" He asked. "Let's go upstairs to my hotel room."

Kate grinned but shook her head. "No," she stated. "Let's go to *mine*."

She'd barely touched her salad but she didn't care. She hadn't paid for it. As she stood up from the table, she downed the rest of her wine. She wasn't going to let *that* go to waste. The wine warmed her body as it slipped down into her stomach. She set the glass down on the table and looked at Gerard who was waiting for her just a few steps away.

His excitement was palpable in the air, his eyes darting all over the room as he tapped his foot against the floor. Kate smiled up to him, took hold of his hand, and led him out into the lobby. Luckily for her, an elevator was already waiting for them. They rode it up to her floor in silence.

Gerard followed her out of the elevator, his hands touching her hips and stomach from behind. Kate felt her body react to his touch, sending shivers all over her skin.

When her door was unlocked, she stepped inside, dragging Gerard with her. His lips went to her neck, kissing the tender skin there. Kate felt her whole body shudder as her head leaned back and her mouth opened. A moan was waiting in the hollow of her throat, begging to be released.

Gerard's hands wound around her stomach, his fingers stretching out past the waistband of her underwear. Kate let her hands wind around the back of Gerard's neck, grabbing fistfuls of his hair, tugging on it gently.

Before they went any further, Kate knew she needed to put down some ground rules. She tried to worm her way out of Gerard's grasp, slipping her hips between his hands as she turned around to face him, but he wouldn't let her go.

The passion was deep in his eyes, a fire burning inside them as his hands roamed up and down her body. Gerard bit his bottom lip as he stared down at Kate, his chest rising and falling as his excitement grew.

Kate could feel it against her thigh, getting larger with every beat of his heart. Her pussy clenched as she felt it.

She knew she needed to get the upper hand soon. Otherwise, Gerard was going to take over and she wasn't going to have a good time. There was a certain way Kate liked these encounters to go, and the man being in charge wasn't her idea of fun. Most men liked being in charge, though, so there was often a power struggle involved.

Kate managed to slip out of his grasp and walked backward to the bed, her eyes connected with his.

"Listen," she whispered. "We're going to do this *my* way."

Gerard followed her, still biting on his bottom lip. "And what is your way?"

"With me in charge," Kate said, staring up at him as he towered over her.

A soft, gentle laugh came out between Gerard's lips but Kate didn't have enough time to question him on it. He leaned down and kissed her, letting their lips dance together for a moment. Then his tongue found its way into her mouth, exploring her, and Gerard's hands returned to her body.

Kate was too taken aback by his lips to say anything. The passion was taking over, driving her now. Every inch of her body was lighting on fire and there was nothing she could do to stop it.

Without thinking, she wound her arms around the back of his neck and pulled him down to the bed behind her, letting his body fall on top of hers.

Chapter Seven

Harder

THEY'D MADE OUT ON the bed for what felt like hours. As much as Kate enjoyed a good kissing session, her lips were starting to get sore. She could feel the skin starting to chafe around the tops of her lip.

Somehow she managed to break away from Gerard's eager mouth and held him at arm's length. She looked into his eyes and steadied her breath.

"Enough," she whispered. "I want you. Now."

Gerard didn't need any more prompting than that. He leaped off the bed with the energy that only a young man had and began unbuttoning his shirt.

Kate could feel the excitement rising in her stomach as she peeled off her cotton clothes. They floated off her body and careened down to the floor in gentle ripples and waves. Her eyes stayed connected with Gerard's as they both shed their clothes.

In the bottom corners of her vision, she could see Gerard's bare chest glistening in the dim light of her hotel room. He barely had any hairs there—his body was just too young for them to have formed yet.

Kate tried not to think about it as she stood there in her underwear, staring into his blue eyes. He was looking back at her with such ferocity, adrenaline pumping through his body as he began to engage in what was probably one of his first one-night stands.

His hands cemented themselves on her bare hips and began to push her back to the bed. Kate wanted to fight against him, to gain control of the situation, but she knew she wasn't going to be able to win with brute force.

So, she did the only thing she could think of. She wrapped her arms around his neck and stood on the very tips of her toes. As she balanced there in his arms, she pressed her lips onto the edges of his ear, gently tugging at his skin with her teeth.

"I'm going to fuck you senseless," she whispered.

It gave him pause, at least for a moment. It was enough time for Kate to turn their bodies so she would be on top. All she had to do was gently push him down and she'd be able to have her way with him.

Gerard wasn't going to play games with her, though.

"No," he growled. "*I'm* going to fuck *you* senseless."

He pried her hands away from his neck and twisted their bodies around as he held onto her wrists. Then, without saying a word, he threw Kate back down onto the bed.

The mattress bounced beneath her, sending her body rocking through the air. She could only watch as Gerard climbed on top of her, his eyes alight with passion.

Kate couldn't help but feel a little disappointed. This was why she never bothered with men. This was why she kept to pleasing herself. Not only could men never give her the kind of orgasms she could give herself, but they refused to let women take the lead.

Who cared about Kate's enjoyment? Certainly not Gerard. Kate felt his lips connect with her neck, wet and slobbery as he trailed his tongue down her skin in an attempt to tease her.

This is why you don't fuck boys, she scolded herself. *You need a man who knows when to step back and let the woman take control. These young boys don't know shit.*

As much as she wanted to lie there and complain about him, she knew she had to be active in this activity. She put her arms around his waist and let her nails dig into his skin, trying to ramp up the heat between them.

Even though it wasn't the encounter that Kate wanted, she knew she should enjoy it at the very least. She buried her head into Gerard's shoulder as he kissed up and down her neck. Having a man's weight pressing down onto her body was distracting—so distracting that she was barely aroused.

It was only when Gerard shoved his hand down Kate's underwear that everything started to perk up. Her breaths became shallow as his fingers brushed up and down her lips, teasing her as he continued kissing every available inch of her body.

Her stomach turned into a big, knotted ball of energy and adrenaline. Her heartbeat was pumping through her whole body, making every piece of her thump loudly. She could hear it in her ears, feel it in her fingers, and see her heart beating behind her ribs.

Gerard's fingers slipped past her lower lips, suddenly enveloped by her warmth. Kate gasped and threw her head back as his fingers plunged deeper, exploring her. Gerard followed her head, putting his lips on the hollow of her throat as he continued to push his fingers deeper inside.

A soft moan came out of her mouth, whispering on her breath as she arched her back. Gerard pushed his fingers into her, sinking into her depths, before slowly withdrawing them. He lifted his head from her neck and stared into her eyes.

The mood changed in the room, then. There was something in his eyes. They had softened, warmed up to her... and Kate didn't like it. It almost looked like he was falling in love with her. Kate felt her stomach churn as she looked into his deep blue eyes.

Is he going to... make love to me? Kate felt her heart pound, but instead of excitement, it was dread.

*

The last time a man had made love to her was when she was still married. When they were happy, sneaking kisses while their infant daughter took a nap. Kate didn't want to be reminded of those times; she'd evolved past that need. It wasn't a place she wanted to go back to, nor was it a mindset she particularly cared for.

Back then, she'd been controlled by her emotions. If anything bad ever happened in her life, she would just curl up into a ball and sob. When her husband left her, it took her days to peel herself off the bathroom floor.

Stop, Kate thought.

She couldn't be thinking about this while she was trying to fuck someone. The only thing she could do was push the thoughts away and try to focus on the moment.

Gerard climbed off of her and hooked his thumbs into his underwear. Within a second they were on the floor beside the bed. Kate couldn't stop herself from looking at the space between his legs.

There was his reason for being so cocky. He was at least seven inches long, with impressive girth, and huge balls. Of course, balls didn't mean anything to her, but to men, they were weirdly important.

His cock was standing tall in the air, aiming right for her pussy. Kate quickly shimmied her underwear down and spread her legs, inviting him inside.

Gerard didn't need any more prompting. Without a word, he put his knees between Kate's legs and positioned his cock between her lips. She felt his cockhead touching her, about to delve inside, when he started to kiss her again.

Kate wanted to groan, to roll over and get away from him, but she was already here and she wanted the fuck she'd been promised. For a moment, she considered wrapping her legs around his waist and flipping him over so she could ride him for a while, but she knew that wouldn't go down well.

Gerard took his time, easing his cock in with gentle thrusts, as he continued to kiss all over her chest and neck. Kate made all the right noises when he kissed her nipples, her neck, and her lips. But she wasn't really feeling it. He was going too slow. His cock was controlled, thrusting in and out of her so gently she could barely feel his length.

When she finally felt his pelvis pressing against hers, Kate woke herself up from her almost-bored daze. His cock was deep inside of her, almost splitting her apart. Kate stared up into his eyes, confused at what he was waiting for.

Gerard looked at her so lovingly as his hand brushed a strand of her hair away from her face.

"You're so beautiful," he purred, before burying his head between her neck and shoulders.

It only took a moment for his elbows to dig into the mattress beneath them, and then he started to thrust. Kate had been expecting something fantastic, something that made her whole body shiver and convulse, but instead she felt nothing.

His hips were basically still as he gave out the tiniest of thrusts. Kate tried to grip onto his hips and pull them toward her body, forcing him to thrust harder, but he was immovable. Nothing she did was going to get him to change.

Not only did he have a huge ego on him, but he also thought that his way of having sex was the best and there was no other way to do it. Kate could've cried. All she wanted was a little more action, a little more passion. But it seemed that Gerard was only capable of mushy, sweet sex.

That wasn't something that Kate wanted to endure. She wanted to force him off of her, to kick him to the end of the bed and ride him into oblivion, but the best she could hope for was a quick finish and an easy exit.

He continued thrusting, boring Kate so much that she almost fell asleep. His rhythmic thrusts were like being rocked to sleep. Kate struggled to keep her eyes open as Gerard's lips continued to smooch every inch of her skin.

Only when he started to thrust faster and harder did Kate start to feel some kind of electricity between her legs. Gerard's cock plunged in and out of her, thrusting harder and harder with every second that passed.

Kate's legs broke out into tingles as he fucked her harder. Her body rocked back and forth on the bed as her stomach started to clench. Finally, this was a fucking that she could get behind. She dug her fingers into his hips, helping his thrust harder and faster. Kate hoped that he would last a little longer, giving her time to at least edge closer to the sweet nirvana waiting for her.

She felt it starting to happen. Gerard's body trembled against hers as his cock began to pulse inside of her. She felt it rising up to the top of her pelvis and then, within a second, his cum filled her.

Kate let her hands drop from his body. Defeat wasn't even the word for how she felt. All she could think about was what a waste of time this had been. She wasn't even sweating, the sex was that boring.

Why had she bothered to sleep with a sexy young European when all he wanted to do was make love like a little bitch? Kate stayed still until

Gerard had recovered from his explosive orgasm and rolled away from her.

When he was on his back, panting like crazy and looking up to the ceiling, Kate let out a heavy sigh as she sat up and perched on the edge of the bed. She was done here. There was no getting back the evening and she wasn't going to waste any more time in his company.

She began to get dressed immediately, pulling her underwear over her feet as quickly as she could. Looking down at her hands, she realized that they weren't even shaking anymore. All of the adrenaline had been wiped out of her system and replaced with utter boredom.

"Sweet Kate," Gerard said, barely able to squeeze the words out between his ragged breaths. "Where are you going?"

Kate looked over her shoulder to him and raised her left eyebrow high up on her forehead. "I'm not going anywhere," she said. "This is my hotel room. *You're* the one leaving. Get dressed. Now."

Gerard managed to prop his body up on his elbow and shook his head as he stared at her through his blurry, foggy eyes.

"I'm serious," Kate said. "Get dressed."

"So, you used me?" Gerard asked. "You had me make love to you like that and now you're kicking me out?"

Kate stared at him, unable to believe that a man could be that clueless. "I'm sorry," she sighed. "What part of that do you think was fun for me?"

Gerard frowned at her as if he suddenly couldn't speak English anymore. He shook his head from side to side as his mouth opened and closed wordlessly.

"I didn't cum," Kate snapped. "I could barely even feel you thrusting. I wasn't sure if you were trying to fuck me or fall asleep on me."

Gerard scowled at her. "I was too gentle?"

"Yeah," Kate said. "And now I'm done with you. So leave."

Gerard took a moment to steady his breaths and clear his eyes. Kate tried not to pay any attention to him as she gathered her clothes.

What a fucking joke, Kate thought bitterly. *And for a moment there I thought this vacation would be exactly what I needed. But no. Of course not. Just another disappointing fuck from a disappointing man.*

Gerard's hand clamped around her wrist and whirled her around. Shocked, her mouth hung open as she looked down at him. The passion was back in his eyes again, but the look didn't excite Kate.

"I'm not done with you," he said sharply. "Get back on the bed."

Kate tried to wrench her hand out of his grasp but he refused to let go. Just as she frowned down at him, Gerard yanked her back down to the bed and clamped his fingers around the waistband of her underwear.

In one, swift motion, he yanked them off, leaving them hanging around her ankles. Gerard put his fingers straight on her clitoris, clearly not fucking around now.

Kate was shocked. The tender, loving man was gone. He'd been replaced by an animal that knew what he wanted and took it. Kate allowed herself to relax on the bed as she felt Gerard's fingers circle around her clit.

"I'm not letting you leave until you cum," he said as he leaned his face down between her legs.

Kate parted them to make room for his head and within a couple of seconds, felt his lips and tongue against her most tender spot. Kate's eyes instantly closed as she felt him lapping at her, his warm tongue saturating her with his saliva and gently licking her engorged clit.

It didn't take long for her body to start reacting. Finally, she was starting to feel something. Her legs kept twitching as he licked and sucked at her, clearly shocked at his pussy eating skills. It didn't take her stomach long to start clenching.

Kate had soon forgotten about all of her complaints. With Gerard's mouth around her pussy, there was nothing in the world that could have distracted her.

As he drove her ever closer to orgasm, she grabbed fistfuls of his hair and tugged on it, her clenching legs wrapped around his shoulders. She couldn't help herself. Her whole body was taken over with heat and sweat as he continued to work on her.

Kate bucked her hips, pressing Gerard's lips against her clit harder. The pleasure was almost too much for her as she ground her body against his face, biting down on her lip to stop her from screaming.

The sweat was streaming off her body and strands of Gerard's hair were breaking off in her fingers. Kate didn't care, though. She held onto him tightly as hot, electric waves rolled through her limbs.

She was close. She could feel it. She'd lost control of her muscles as they tensed up, twitching and jerking around Gerard's body. Her stomach was burning, turning her whole body unbearably hot.

And then a sharp, loud *oh!* broke out of Kate's mouth. A long, heavy sigh followed. Her bottom lip quivered as her whole body started to tense and release, shaking all the way down to her very core.

Too weak to hold onto his head anymore, Kate let go of Gerard's hair and let her hands fall down to her sides. Her whole body was shaking as she lay there, her eyes staring up to the ceiling with a wide smile on her lips.

Gerard came up beside her, a light shine on his lips. "Are you satisfied?"

Kate could only nod in reply. Her breaths were rushed and ragged and there was no way she was going to be able to talk for another ten minutes or so. The only thing she could do is stay there, on her back, feeling the warm, happy tingles running through her veins.

Chapter Eight

Take control

WHEN KATE OPENED HER eyes, she was surprised to see sunlight beaming into her hotel room. She sat up in her bed and heard the sound of sheets rustling around her. Looking down, she saw that she was tucked into bed.

As far as Kate remembered, she didn't get into bed last night. She'd been on her back, naked on the bed, and she'd just closed her eyes for a moment.

Kate turned to her right, looking at the other side of the bed, and she saw Gerard's naked, smooth back. Of course, the romantic gentleman had helped her into bed and spent the night beside her.

As much as Kate wanted to roll her eyes and tut at his behavior, she couldn't help but be thankful. If she'd stayed naked above the covers, she would have woken up in the middle of the night freezing cold and pissed off. At least she'd gotten a good night's sleep, even if they did share a bed reluctantly.

It's no big deal, Kate told herself as she pushed the covers off her legs. *He satisfied me last night. The least I could do is let him stay the night. Besides, this isn't my house. This is a god damn hotel.*

Memories of the previous night washed over Kate, sending shivers down her spine. The night had been a bust at first, but somehow Gerard had managed to win her over with his excellent tongue.

Kate didn't usually like to sleep with a man more than one night in a row, but for those kinds of orgasms, she wouldn't mind giving it another shot. However, she'd definitely have to take control this time.

As she got up out of the bed, she tried to remember if she'd brought handcuffs with her. While it was always good to be prepared—and Kate usually was—she didn't think she'd thought *that* far ahead.

Shame, she thought. *That would be a perfect way to get him to relinquish control.*

Kate found a bathrobe in the bathroom and wrapped it around her body. She was comfortable being naked but it was damn cold. The air conditioning didn't have a temperature control on it, so there was no way she could bump it up a couple of degrees. A bathrobe would have to do.

As she made her way over to the desk, where her laptop bag was placed, she looked over to Gerard. He was still fast asleep, his chest rising and falling slowly.

She was torn. On the one hand, she didn't want to just dismiss a man because his ego was a little inflated. On the other hand, she knew that no good could come from giving him a second chance. He'd already pleased her well enough. What more could he give? He wasn't going to change his ways just for a quick fuck.

Kate tried to push her thoughts away as she pulled her laptop out of the bag and began to set it up. She was on vacation, cut off from the rest of the world, but that didn't mean she was barred from also checking her emails.

Nothing could have stopped her. Checking her emails was the only way she was going to be able to keep up with the company. She didn't want to go back to work and find out she was completely behind everything. Knowing the ins and outs of what was going on was the only way she was going to protect her job.

As she waited for her laptop to boot, she sorted the tangled charger cable and plugged it into the wall, and leaned back in the wicker chair. Her laptop was a couple of years old and was overloaded with crap. It always took a lifetime to load everything.

Kate could have bought her own work laptop easily, but she didn't want to bother. Besides, her job seemed to be on the line these days, and if she got fired she'd have to hand over the work laptop, even if she bought it.

There was no way she was going to spend a load of money for a fancy machine only to have it taken away. And Kate had a funny feeling that it would happen since her bosses hated her so damn much. Not only did they hate her, but they were more sexist than anyone else she'd met in her life.

Before she had a chance to go down the rabbit hole in her own mind, her laptop booted up, revealing her plain blue desktop background.

Kate lunged forward and immediately loaded up her email client, hoping that her laptop would be able to connect to the hotel's internet.

She had to scroll through all the crap for ages, trying to get back to the oldest unread emails she had. Most of it was useless, just company-wide notifications that she'd been included in. Then there were conversations from her department that she'd be given reports about when she got back. She glossed over it all, looking for anything from people above her.

Finally, she found something. Her boss, Walter Harpe, had sent an email out to all the executives explaining what had happened with her. As she opened the email, a pit opened up in her stomach. She knew this wasn't going to be good.

The first couple of lines were fine, explaining where Kate was and who would be taking over particular tasks of hers until she returned. It was great for her to know who she could turn to when she got back and realized they fucked everything up.

As she kept on going through the emails, she saw them derail into a full-scale bitch about her. All of the men were chiming in, telling each other how awful Kate had been, and how they were so glad to see the back of her.

Of course, none of the women were saying a word. There weren't many of them but they were there, included in the conversation but just sitting by and letting the men talk shit. Kate couldn't blame them, but it still stung. Why weren't they standing up for her? She'd stood up for them multiple times.

Kate tried not to concentrate on it as she gritted her teeth and continued reading through the thread. Of course, the men were just getting worse and worse, calling her an entitled bitch and mocking the way she dressed and even spoke.

A sick taste rose up in her throat as she continued reading. The corners of her mouth turned down as she tasted the bile on the back of her tongue. How could they be so cruel to her? She'd never done anything to them, aside from showing them that women were capable and just as worthy of respect as men.

Kate wanted to slam her laptop shut and force herself to stop reading the awful words, but she couldn't. It was like a drug, constantly pulling her in repeatedly. Kate knew that she couldn't handle reading all this bullshit about herself but she also couldn't stop.

She got to the top of the thread. An email from her boss, Walter, telling the men that Kate was involved in the thread and that she could read everything they'd been saying.

That was dated almost twenty-four hours ago. Kate scowled at that last email, shaking her head slowly.

Of course they stopped, Kate thought angrily. *Of course, they shut up when they realized I could see everything. Fucking cowards.*

Kate leaned back in her chair, staring at the screen as she fiddled with her bottom lip. It was so disgusting what they had said about her, calling her a stupid bitch and an idiot behind her back, but it was even worse that they all shut up when they realized she could see it all.

Just thinking about looking through emails or doing more work made Kate feel even more sick. Her whole body was shaking, nauseous, and totally uncontrolled. Her legs were bouncing up and down as she sat at the table, staring at her blank computer screen.

With nothing else to do, Kate shut her laptop screen and clenched her hands in her lap. What the hell was she supposed to do now? The rage was going to take over her. It was already pulsing through her veins, through her muscles, through her fucking *bones*. How was she going to get herself out of this mess?

Behind her, she could hear Gerard snoring gently. Her eyes drifted over to his sleeping body. It was like a light bulb went off behind her eyes. She might not have had handcuffs on her, but she could tie him up with other things.

It was a naughty thought, but a thought she wanted to follow through with anyway. Kate stood up from the table and climbed up onto the bed, putting her knees on either side of Gerard's legs so she could crawl up his body.

As she was coming toward his face, Gerard stirred and rolled onto his back. His eyes opened gently, peering out at Kate's face above him. It took him a moment to realize what was happening and come out of his dreamy daze.

When he finally woke up properly, he put his hands on Kate's hips and reached his lips up to kiss her. Kate wrenched her head away just in time to dodge the kiss.

“What’s wrong?” Gerard asked, frowning as he let his head relax into the pillow below.

“Nothing,” Kate said, feeling a smile playing on the corners of her lips. “Nothing at all.”

“I don’t understand,” he said, ever so softly. “There’s something in your eyes. What is it?”

“Nothing,” Kate said quickly. “Work stuff. It’s fine.”

Gerard went to open his mouth but Kate didn’t want to hear his words anymore. She leaned down and kissed him, instantly shoving her tongue into his mouth.

When his hands gripped her hips tighter, Kate leaned backward a little and grabbed hold of his wrists. In one, swift motion, she trapped his wrists against the mattress and held them there.

Gerard laughed and moved his head to the left, breaking off the kiss. When Kate leaned back a little more, Gerard looked into her eyes.

“What are you doing?” He asked, his lilted voice rising and falling gently. “Get off me and I’ll fuck you like I did last night.”

He raised his eyebrows then as if that was something that Kate should have wanted. She only stared down at him, shaking her head slowly.

“No, baby,” Kate whispered. “Last night was all you. Today is all me.”

Gerard smiled, unable to believe he was hearing this. “What do you mean?” He asked. “I made you cum. I saw your face.”

Kate rolled her eyes. "But the sex was boring," she said. "This time, we're doing it my way."

Kate climbed off his body and dived into her luggage, sifting through all of her clothes to find the little box of toys she'd brought on vacation with her. She knew there were a couple of rolled-up ties in there. Those would have to do.

When she had the silk in her hands, she jumped back onto the bed. Gerard was already starting to sit up, his eyebrows furrowed so deeply they were covering his blue eyes.

"What are you doing?" He asked.

"Doing what *I* want," Kate said.

Her hand slapped against Gerard's chest, pushing him back into the bed. His arms splayed out at either side of him, giving Kate easy access to tie his wrists to the bed posts.

Once his wrists were tight against the circular poles of wood, Gerard looked up to them, concerned.

"I don't think this will be a good idea," he said. "The man is supposed to b—"

Kate slapped her hand over his mouth. "Don't say what men and women are supposed to do," she snapped. "If I want to ride you, I'm going to ride you."

Gerard continued frowning but he didn't argue. Kate removed her hand from his mouth and threw the covers away from his body.

To her delight, he was already rock hard. She wasn't sure if it was because he had a fantastic case of morning wood, or if he was secretly enjoying what Kate was doing. Either way, she didn't care. There was cock enough for her to use.

She wrapped her hand tightly around his member and jerked him off, bringing her hand up and down slowly as she stared into his eyes. Despite his clear discomfort at the lack of control, he closed his eyes and leaned his head back into the pillows.

Within a couple of seconds, loud moans were coming out of his mouth. Kate couldn't help but smile as she continued to stroke his cock. While he wasn't looking, she positioned herself over his pelvis, and within a second she'd switched her hand for her pussy.

Gerard gasped and threw his head up, looking down at his cock. There, he saw Kate's naked body connected with his. Groaning loudly, he began to buck his hips gently as Kate eased herself down onto him.

She wasn't going to tolerate that. She leaned forward and grabbed his chin, forcing him to stare into her eyes.

"Don't move," she said sternly. "Do. Not. Move."

Kate leaned back on Gerard's cock and began to lift her hips slowly, allowing herself to pause with only Gerard's tip inside, before lowering again. She kept it slow and steady so she could control herself and build the passion slowly.

It looked like love-making at first, but she knew that soon it would turn rough—rougher than Gerard had ever experienced, no doubt. Kate couldn't wait any longer. She began to ride Gerard harder, lifting her whole body with the strength in her thighs.

She kept her eyes open so she could see Gerard's desperate face. It was clear he wanted to grab hold of her and take control, but since his hands were tied above his head, all he could do was thrash his arms as he stared up at Kate.

Within a second she'd leaned down to kiss him—but it wasn't tender, how he'd kissed her the previous night. It was rough, with her tongue shoving into his mouth and lapping around his.

Kate let her hand move up his chest, sliding against his skin, until her fingers found their way around his throat. As she leaned back, still lifting and rising on his cock, she gripped the sides of his neck tightly.

Gerard's eyes bulged out of his head as he stared up at her, helpless. His mouth opened and closed as she continued to ride him. It was like he was too shocked to say anything or even do anything. Kate continued to ride him as she gripped his throat.

Soon she was grinding her hips against his, thrashing and circling her pussy around his cock, screaming out as her head rolled back and her mouth hung open.

When she used his cock how she desired, it was incredible, especially when compared to his pathetic love-making. There was no passion, no fire, not even a little heat.

But now Kate could feel her stomach clenching as she continued to grind him, rubbing her clit against his skin until she was close to climax. With her hand clamped around his throat, Kate felt herself starting to tremble and shake.

She leaned forward, both of her elbows digging into Gerard's chest, and wrapped both of her hands around his neck. With her back slightly arched, she slid her hips back and forth as she humped him.

His cock slipped in and out of her, pushing so deep she could feel his tip flicking against her cervix. The sweet pain of it only made her fuck him harder.

She wanted his cock inside her, deeper and deeper until there was no more room. She thrusted until sweat was careening down her back in long, wet lines. Kate's hair was sticking to her back in thick clumps, snagging at her scalp. She didn't care, though.

The only thing that mattered to her was what was between her legs. Gerard's cock was rock hard, pulsing inside of her, and she knew she didn't have long left to make herself cum. She'd ridden Gerard for too long. Soon he'd spill his seed.

Kate sped up, grinding against him harder, and removed one of her hands from Gerard's neck so she could touch herself. After licking her fingers, saturating them with her saliva, she moved it down to her clit.

It only took a couple of minutes of rubbing for her to feel all of her muscles start to tighten. It was going to happen. Kate's stomach churned but she wasn't going to slow down. She ground her hips against Gerard's harder, pushing herself ever closer to the edge.

Heat washed over her body in waves. Her muscles tensed and released, filling her whole body with adrenaline. Her mouth opened and a soft moan came out as she felt her pussy clamp around Gerard's cock. A second later, he began to moan, too. It was a strangled sound.

Kate let go of his throat as she continued to cum, her whole body shaking and trembling as her muscles contracted. Everything else was secondary to feeling the pleasure pulsing through her body.

It took her a couple of moments to realize that Gerard's cock was still inside her. She put her hands on his stomach and sat up, looking down at him. He was red-faced and covered in sweat, his eyes ablaze.

As Kate moved her pelvis, she felt his semen inside her. Grimacing, she leaned to the right and felt his limp cock slip out of her. The only thing she could do was stay on her back, panting, feeling tremors still rolling through her exhausted body.

Chapter Nine

Butterflies

THE NIGHT CAME ON swiftly for Kate. The whole day had been a blur, really. After her intense orgasm riding Gerard's cock, she hadn't been able to concentrate on anything. At first, she'd wanted to go down to the beach and relax, but getting up out of the bed had been too much for her tired body to handle.

So, she'd spent the entire day in bed, lounging on the dirty sheets. From the bed, she'd watched the sun setting in the sky, turning the whole world orange and red. At least she could see out of the door from the bed. It was better than lying there doing nothing.

When her stomach started to rumble, Kate knew that she had to venture outside into the real world and feed herself. She wasn't even sure if her legs were going to be able to carry her down there. For a moment she thought about ordering room service, but once she'd looked over the lackluster menu she knew she needed to go downstairs.

It took her longer than it should have for her to pull herself out of bed and get dressed. She didn't bother to change her clothes—she just picked up her floaty, cotton clothes, and tossed them onto her body.

As she thought, her legs could barely support her weight at first. Not only had her intense orgasm completely ripped through her muscles, but relaxing in bed all day had seemingly weakened them as well.

By the time she got into the elevator, her stomach was loudly rumbling every couple of seconds. She could feel the hunger eating away at her, a physical pain deep in her stomach.

Kate was glad it was a buffet. She'd be able to eat as much as she liked without having any wait staff looking at her like she was a pig. She ate as much as she could. Meat, vegetables, pasta, even dessert. Everything she liked the look of, she took.

When she was filled to bursting, she leaned back in her chair and sighed heavily. Her eyes drifted across the sea of diners as she thought about her forced vacation.

So far, it wasn't terrible. She'd managed to get herself some sex and, while the first time was a little disappointing, the second time was a lot better. As she sat there, she kept on thinking about poor Gerard.

He'd left her hotel room in such a rush that she hadn't even been able to get his room number from him. Kate couldn't even sit up to watch him scurry out with his clothes clutched in his arms.

The image of that wouldn't leave her mind. The look in his eyes, the terror. Or was it terror? Kate couldn't be sure. There was something there, though, lingering in his eyes as he struggled to collect his things quick enough.

Kate was broken out of her daze long enough to see a familiar face across the dining hall. A group of men—boys, really—were sat around one of the larger tables. Between the heads of thick, dark hair, she could see Gerard's face.

Frowning, she tilted her head to get a better look at him. He was surrounded by his friends but that didn't disguise his face. Something had changed. His skin was pale, his eyes were dark and shadowed, and his smile didn't reach up to his eyes.

Kate couldn't be sure if she'd done that to him, or if it was something else. Had she fucked the life out of him? It seemed like a plausible thing. After all, what else could he have done in the hours since he left her hotel room?

It was only a matter of time until Gerard's eyes met hers. The smile on his lips vanished and his face fell entirely, making his skin look saggy and wrinkled. When his friends saw the look on his face, they rallied around him to see what his problem was.

His unwavering gaze nodded over to Kate. As his friends all turned around to look at her, she realized that he'd told them all about his night. Now there was no doubt in her mind that it was her who had done this to him.

Guilt started to eat away at her as her mind started to think about everything that had happened that morning. Kate knew that she shouldn't have slept with a boy so young, but now that his friends were shaking their heads and ushering Gerard out of the room she couldn't stop feeling like she was in a scene from a movie. All of his friends rallied around him, bringing him away from the nasty woman who took away his innocence.

Kate felt a laugh bubbling up inside of her but she knew she couldn't let it out. Those boys didn't know a good fuck when it got on its knees and sucked their dicks, but she couldn't tell them that either.

When Gerard was old and crusty, he would get it. He'd realize that Kate had done him a favor, showing him what true sex looked like. The knowledge that he wasn't man enough for her comforted her but there was still the little thought in the back of her mind, worried that she'd ruined that boy forever.

Don't sleep with someone so young again, she thought. *Never again. It's not worth it. They're crap in bed, even if they look fantastic.*

Kate knew that she needed to get out of there. The guilt and shame were going to take over soon and she needed to be out of sight of other people to endure it.

She pushed her chair out from under the table and made her way to the elevators, keeping her face turned down to the ground. Usually, she was so confident that nothing could disturb her, but this had.

Those boys were flocking around their friend like he was a hurt little bird, fallen out of the nest. She had never seen men act like that before—only women. Was she such a terrible person that people needed to be protected from her?

Stop, Kate thought desperately. *Stop thinking about it. This is all bullshit.*

Her feet carried her to the elevator faster, her legs rushing to bring her back to the hotel room. A shoulder slammed into her side, forcing her to twist around. Her feet stumbled over each other as she struggled to maintain her balance. Her arms splayed out at either side and grabbed onto the nearest thing she could—a man's arm.

Kate felt his hands grabbing onto her and pulling her up, supporting her weight as she struggled to find her feet. When Kate felt steady, she glanced up at the man that had bumped her off-course. His jet black hair was covered in gel and smoothed back over his head, with a couple of strands falling down over his deep, brown eyes.

"I'm sorry," he said, his plump lips widening to reveal his white teeth. "Didn't mean to send you flying."

Kate couldn't recognize his accent but it certainly wasn't European. It sounded like the man was from South America, the beautiful lilted tones accentuating his English.

"Are you okay?" He asked, raising his eyebrows as he stared at her.

Kate looked over his face and couldn't help but smile. He had a crooked nose that was rather large for his face, and a wide, chiseled jaw that stuck out on either side of his face. Thick, black stubble covered his cheeks and jaw where he hadn't shaved in a couple of days.

As Kate looked him over, the only thing she could think was that he was certainly more age-appropriate. He looked to be at least in his thirties, maybe even forties. Totally acceptable and experienced enough for Kate. A smile burst out onto her lips as she thought about how great his face would look, shoved between her legs.

"It's fine," she said sweetly. "Thanks for catching me."

She wasn't about to stand around and talk to him, though. As much as she was attracted to him, she knew that she was too ashamed to even bother trying to pick him up. The best she could hope for was that she'd see him around some time.

Kate nodded to him before making her way to the elevators. As she waited for them to come, she tried not to look over her shoulder to see if the man was still there.

Just thinking about him set her heart thumping hard in her chest. The elevator doors opened and Kate rushed inside. As she turned around to press the button, she saw the black-haired man standing in the middle of the lobby, his eyes focused on her.

Kate felt the heat rush up into her cheeks as she covered her smiling mouth and turned her eyes down to the floor. As the doors closed, she felt butterflies erupt in her stomach just thinking about that beautiful, black-haired man.

Chapter Ten

Like an animal

When Kate awoke in her bed the next morning, she instantly felt disappointment wash over her. Her eyes hadn't even had enough time to adjust to the bright light, or to blink away the blur. It was harrowing and heavy, weighing down on her shoulders like a weighted blanket wrapped around her neck.

The worst part of it all was that Kate was starting to doubt herself. Every choice she'd ever made, every man that she'd ever slept with, it was all flashing behind her eyes as she constantly thought about it.

She threw her legs over the side of the bed and rubbed her tired eyes. Nothing would stop the thoughts rushing through her head, no matter how much she tried not to think about them.

What she really needed was a distraction, something to get her out of the hotel and away from her mistakes. Since she was on vacation, she knew she wouldn't have to deal with the mistakes forever, but the quicker she could get out and about and forget all about Gerard, the better it would be for her.

Kate turned on the small, flat-screen TV at the end of her bed as she tried to find clothes, listening to the English weather channel. She had no idea what she was going to do, but she knew she had to do something and get away from Gerard.

He was just a boy, there was no doubt in her mind that he would just sit around by the pool and drink himself into a stupor. She needed to go out into the world and explore a little.

The weather channel told her it was going to be a blisteringly hot day. Kate found herself a wide-brimmed hat and all-white clothes that were breathable and comfortable. Another shirt, this time it was made of linen, with her swimsuit beneath. She paired it with patterned pants, cut off just below her knees.

It wasn't the style she usually went for—making her look like she was from Spain or something—but she just needed something comfortable to wear. She wasn't used to the heat.

Kate didn't even want to stay in the hotel long enough for breakfast, scared she'd run into Gerard somewhere along the way. Instead, she made her way to the back of the hotel and onto the beach.

The last time she was there, she'd seen a small pedestrian path leading up to a market. Kate meandered up the hilly path and let her eyes drift over the sight.

Dozens of stalls covered with canvas roofs were scattered around the area. Most of them were selling clothes, hats, and sunglasses, but some of them were selling American magazines and even books. Kate let herself wander around for a while, staring down at the wares.

The farther into the market she got, the more she managed to see of it. At first she'd thought it was only this area, but she could see stalls lined up for miles, all of them standing on the edge of the beach.

It was a prime location for it, after all. People would come up off the beach having forgotten something important and they'd instantly be drawn into the market stalls. Once they started spending, it would be impossible to stop. Before they knew it, they'd have spent hundreds of dollars, all on junk.

Kate allowed herself to peruse the stalls but she knew she wouldn't buy anything. Half of the designer items were fakes and she wasn't about to waste her money on that, especially not considering she could buy the real thing at home if she really wanted it.

It was just nice to get out, to be around people, and not wonder if they were staring at her. Gossip spread quickly—she was all too aware of that—but she hadn't expected to be on the wrong end of gossip on vacation.

Kate sighed as she walked through the stalls, touching the scarves and hats as she passed. The crowds were growing thicker as it grew closer to lunch. Desperate, hungry eyes were all looking for a good deal.

When Kate got elbowed and shoved out of the way by some brown-haired bimbo with massive fake tits, she knew it was time to find something else to do. She took a detour away from the market and found herself on a strip. There were a couple of small grocery stores, along with bookstores and clothing boutiques.

Kate had no idea that such a quaint, honest place was so close to the tourist traps. She kept on walking down the quiet road as she tried to find a small place she'd be able to stop and grab something to eat.

Before she knew it, Kate had wandered completely away from the tourist areas and found herself amongst the locals. Although she was a little worried about finding her way back to the hotel, she tried to enjoy herself as she took in the sights.

Kate rounded a corner, trying to make her way back to the hotel when she ran into a hard body. She felt herself falling backward as her arms swung out at her sides. The man's hands clamped down on her arms and anchored her to the floor.

When she looked up, she was shocked to see Gerard looking down at her. He instantly withdrew his hands and the corners of his lips curled down into disgust.

"What is your problem?" Kate blurted.

She couldn't have stopped the words, even if she'd tried. They just rolled right out of her mouth. Gerard's eyes widened as he looked down at her, frowning.

"Well?" Kate asked, not quite as forceful as before. "What's your problem?"

"I don't have a problem," Gerard said quietly. "You're the one with the problem, lady."

Kate sighed and put her hands on her hips. She hadn't approached this well, but the shock of running into him had caused her mouth to run.

If she hadn't been taken by surprise, she might have been able to form her words a little better. It hadn't worked out that way, though.

"Clearly not," Kate snapped. "You and your little friends couldn't have run out of there quick enough when you saw me. You scared?"

The way Gerard backed away told her that he was afraid. Whatever she'd done in their hotel room, it had clearly frightened him to his very core. Kate wanted to pity him but she couldn't bring herself to.

If he couldn't handle her, it was his problem, not hers. He was the one who wanted to sleep with her, he was the one who wanted to spend the night with her.

"No one is scared," Gerard said.

Kate could have sworn she heard him whimper. She wasn't going to stand around and listen to his bullshit. She rolled her eyes and stormed past him, muttering *whatever.*

Gerard wasn't going to let her get away that easily, though. He grabbed her wrist and spun her around before she could get away. Suddenly she was in his arms, staring up at him. His blue eyes bored into hers, intense and bright.

"No one is scared," he said. "I'll make love to you again to prove it."

Kate tried to remove herself from his grip but he wouldn't let go. Sighing, Kate placed her arms on his shoulders as she spoke.

"You don't want to do this," Kate said. "You didn't enjoy our time together and that's fine. Some men can't handle me. It's a fact. It's nothing to be ashamed of."

Gerard bristled at that. "I'm not scared," he stated. "I'm not ashamed. I'll make love to you. Tonight. Eight. My hotel room. Room seven-five-one."

Kate tried to make herself look as sincere as possible. "You don't have to do this," she said softly.

"Don't tell me anything," Gerard said, raising his voice. "I'll do what I want."

Then he let go of Kate, almost throwing her away from him, and turned on his heels to storm away. Kate wanted to rush after him, to try and comfort him and tell him that he didn't need to do this, but she knew it would fall on deaf ears.

Despite his reservations, Kate was looking forward to the evening. Gerard wasn't a good match for her, but his cock was fantastic. She considered telling him that he should be a penis model so women around the world could enjoy his gift, but she had a feeling he wouldn't be receptive to that.

What a shame, Kate thought as she strutted down the street. *I'd love to have my own copy of his cock. All the fun I could have...*

Before she turned the corner, heading back to the market so she could find her way back to the hotel, she looked behind her. She could see Gerard storming down the street. His shoulders were hunched over and his fists were clenched.

Kate knew that whatever was going on inside his head wasn't good, but that was none of her concern. He was a big boy and he knew what he was doing. She'd given him an out and he'd refused. There was nothing else to do but look forward to her evening of string-free sex.

Later that night, Kate was dressed in a silk cocktail dress, standing outside Gerard's door. She leaned on the door frame and held her fist up to the door, waiting for a moment before knocking.

She glanced down to herself, where her legs were on show through the slits on either side of her dress, and let her eyes drift down her skin all the way to her toes. Glittery white shoes were wrapped around her feet, forcing her to stand on the tips of her toes.

Even though they were uncomfortable, she knew they made her legs and ass look incredible. That was all that mattered because those shoes would be on the floor soon.

Kate let her knuckles tap against the door slowly and carefully. Behind the door, she could hear Gerard stumbling over his own feet as he rushed to greet her.

When he opened the door, Kate looked up to him with an easy, carefree smile on her lips. Gerard drank in her appearance, his eyes drifting down her toned body, his eyes bulging and his mouth popping open.

"You look..." He couldn't finish his sentence.

Kate brushed past him, letting herself into his room. "I know," she said.

She walked into the middle of the room and set her small purse in front of the TV. Standing there, she looked over her shoulder at Gerard. He was still standing by the door, staring out into the hallway with the door wide open.

This wasn't a good sign. He wasn't eager, or willing. Kate stopped posing and let her body relax. She turned on her heels and took a couple of steps toward him.

"Gerard," she said gently.

He whipped his head around and stared into her eyes. "Did I allow you to use my name?"

His eyes had changed. There was passion in them, intense fire that pooled out into his face. His stern mouth was pressed into a thin line. A shudder went through Kate's body, undulating down to her pussy, as she stared at him.

Gerard slammed the hotel door shut and strutted toward her, moving in large purposeful strides. When he was within arms reach of her, he grabbed her throat.

Kate gasped as she felt his fingers connect with her skin, pressing into her flesh. She leaned back as his hands dug into her, his body careening forward to stare menacingly into her eyes.

"You don't speak unless I tell you to," Gerard snapped. "You don't move unless I tell you to. You don't do anything until I tell you to. Do you understand?"

Kate stayed perfectly still, staring up into his beautiful blue eyes. Her whole body was shivering, breaking out into goosebumps. She could feel her pulse in her crotch as her juices seeped into her underwear.

Whatever reservations she had before went right out the window. Gerard had realized what kind of atmosphere she needed and he was stepping up into that role perfectly.

Usually, she liked to be the one to dominate, to humiliate, to do whatever she liked with... But she was willing to switch for Gerard and his perfect cock. She was willing to be the submissive, just this once, so he could see just how great the sex could be.

The bubbly, excited feeling brewing in her stomach told her that it was going to be fantastic. She could feel her legs turning to jelly beneath her as Gerard pushed his body against hers. His large, erect cock pressed against her stomach, pulsing softly with the beats of his heart.

Kate leaned her neck back, feeling his fingers tighten around her, and stared into his eyes. She was relinquishing control, giving him everything he needed to do this right.

Gerard pushed her back toward the bed. Kate kept her strides strong and sure-footed, desperate not to fall over herself and look like a fool. When she felt her legs press against the edge of the mattress, she stopped moving.

He wasn't done with her yet, though. He continued to push her, forcing her body down onto the bed. Kate felt herself flying through the air before bouncing down into the sheets. Her dress flew around her legs, revealing her bare thighs.

Gerard stood over her, positioned himself between her legs, and he stared down to her. Silently, he began to undress himself. He was only wearing a plain t-shirt and some jeans, but the way he ripped the clothes from his body made Kate shiver.

Not wanting to piss him off, she stayed perfectly still as she'd been instructed. Gerard smiled down to her as he watched her, his eyes drifting over her body.

Her chest hitched up and down, her breaths ragged. Gerard was making her wait, moving his hands ever so slowly up to the neck of his shirt. When his fingers were clasped around it, he tugged it up over his head and shoulders.

When his bare chest was revealed, Kate felt her heart skip a beat. She wanted to reach up and touch him, to pull his heavy body down on top of hers, but she couldn't. She'd been told to stay still and that's exactly what she should be doing, never mind her wants.

Gerard stripped down until he was fully naked, his cock standing tall in the air. He leaned over her, his hands aiming for her shoulders. Kate felt her whole body shiver in anticipation.

His fingers gently peeled away the straps of her dress. Kate arched her back to help him remove the dress, but she kept her arms by her sides as she watched, open-mouthed and wide-eyed.

Her stomach was in knots as she felt the dress slide away from her body, caressing her thighs and calves as it slipped off. Gerard leaned over her and moved his face down to her stomach.

Within an instant his tongue was lapping at her skin, heading down to the waistband of her lacy black underwear. Gerard's teeth snapped around the material and pulled on it, yanking her underwear off her.

Kate shuddered violently and her eyes slipped shut, letting the sensations on her skin take over. It was all she could think about—the way his breath misted against her skin as he tugged the material off her.

She managed to open her eyes just in time to see Gerard remove her underwear from between his teeth and toss them over his shoulder. A huge grin came onto her lips as she stared up at him. She felt like a kid at Christmas, eagerly waiting for her treat.

Gerard didn't say a word to her as he leaned down again, his hands cementing themselves on her hips. He lifted Kate's body up, letting her struggle to support her own head, before turning her over.

Her stomach dropped into the mattress, bouncing around as Gerard let his hands grab her cheeks. When she felt his fingers parting her cheeks, her breaths caught in her lungs.

Hot, electric tingles shot down her stomach as she felt his fingers push inside her pussy. Panting, barely able to stop herself from squirming in delight, she clenched her fists closed and dug her nails into her palms.

"You're soaked," Gerard breathed. "You really like this, don't you? You dirty slut."

A throaty moan escaped Kate's mouth, and another shudder took hold of her. She didn't have time to sit and think about it, though. Gerard dipped down, aligning his hips with hers. Kate felt something warm and large at her lower lips. She realized that he was pressing his cock against her, ready to enter.

Kate could feel him struggling, the angle was just all wrong. Kate slipped her feet down to the floor and raised her ass into the air, making it easier for him to enter. She closed her eyes and silently hoped that Gerard would slam into her from behind and berate her for moving.

Gerard only eased his cock inside and suppressed a gasp. Kate felt a wave of disappointment wash over her. She tried not to let it ruin her mood as she felt Gerard pushing deeper inside of her.

When his pelvis was pressed against her ass, she knew the fun was about to begin. He withdrew his cock slowly until only the tip was inside. Then he slammed into her, rocking their bodies forward on the bed.

Kate's eyes popped open in shock and a moan burst out of her mouth. Her hands searched blindly over the bed covers, trying to find a piece of ruffled cloth to hold onto. Gerard wasn't holding back. He withdrew his cock again, a slight hiss coming from between his teeth, before slamming inside her again.

Kate could feel her whole body turning hot, her skin starting to cover itself in sweat. Gerard was speeding up behind her, withdrawing his cock before thrusting it all the way inside again. Kate's body was rocking back and forth on the bed in a slow rhythm as her mouth opened and closed, moans trying to escape.

Gerard's hands cemented themselves on her hips as he began to pound her. The sound of his cock slipping in and out of her pussy filled the room, along with the soft moans and sighs that Gerard's mouth made.

Tension built in Kate's stomach, gently rising as Gerard continued to fuck her. Hard, harsh thrusts propelled her body forward, rocking her on the bed. His cock filled every inch of her pussy, slipping in and out of her, joined with low grunts from Gerard.

All of the muscles in her body started to tense. Her mind ran away from her, slipping into a black void where no thoughts could escape.

The only thing she could think about was Gerard's cock, pushing in and out of her with ease.

Her whole body trembled as her muscles continued to clench, making her whole body rigid. She could feel the orgasm riding like a wave as Gerard pumped behind her, his skin slapping against hers noisily. Kate's mouth opened, unable to hold back the moans.

Gerard increased his speed, slamming into her quicker and quicker, as Kate's pussy tightened around his cock. Kate's rigid body kept on tensing until her muscles were sore and cramping.

And then it rolled over her. A wash of ecstasy and pleasure undulating down her body as Gerard continued to fuck her. Her spine tingled as she felt every nerve in her body firing. All of her muscles tensed and released in a soothing rhythm.

Gasps and moans seeped out of her mouth. Above her, Gerard was inhaling through his teeth as Kate's pussy clenched around his cock in a vice-like grip.

It only took a couple of seconds before he came, his cock pulsing madly as his semen spurted inside of Kate's pussy. Both of them moaned, covered and slick with sweat, as their bodies relaxed and slowed.

When Gerard withdrew, Kate could feel an emptiness inside of her. It was like she'd molded herself to him and now that he wasn't inside of her anymore, she felt the loss.

She could barely move, her whole body shaking as her muscles continued to twinge. The only thing she could do was roll onto her back and look up to the ceiling. Gerard collapsed next to her on the bed, barely able to catch his breath. They stayed there for a while, in silence, sweating out the last of their encounters.

It only took a couple of minutes for Gerard to get up from the bed and start putting his clothes on. Kate leaned onto her elbows, her breaths still ragged, and watched as he hurried.

"What's wrong?"

"I can't," Gerard snapped. "I just... I can't do this."

Kate frowned. "Do what? Have sex?"

"Like this," Gerard waved his hands around the room, his pants pulled up to his mid-thighs. "It's not lovemaking. It's just animalistic and cruel and I can't do it."

Kate wanted to roll her eyes but she didn't. She kept her mouth shut.

"It's just not for me," Gerard said, his voice cracking. "I'd really appreciate it if you just left. Please."

Kate didn't need to be told twice. She tried not to get upset as she gathered up her clothes. His words had cut her, though. Who was he to say that it was cruel to have sex this way? He had been consenting and she hadn't pushed him.

But, if it wasn't for him, she wasn't going to force him to do something he wasn't comfortable with. As she left his hotel room, fully dressed but still covered in sweat, she held her head up high as she trotted down the hallway and headed back to her own room.

Chapter Eleven

Everybody knows

THE WALK OF SHAME hit Kate hard. She'd only been on her vacation for a couple of days and she'd already made it awkward. How could she show her face in the hotel, knowing that Gerard and all his little friends would be spreading gossip about her? He'd already done it once, there was nothing stopping him from doing it a second time.

As she opened her hotel room door, she tried to tell herself that it didn't matter. She'd only be there for a little while and she would never have to see these people again. The thoughts didn't make her feel better, though. For the next couple of weeks, she'd have to tolerate seeing Gerard in the hallways, in the hotel lobby, on the beach, everywhere around her.

Once she was back in the room, she got herself showered and changed to go to bed. As she lay there, staring up at the ceiling, she couldn't stop her mind from wondering about all the things she'd done wrong. She never should have slept with a man so quickly, nor should she have chosen a man staying at the same hotel. These were rookie mistakes that she should have avoided.

No matter how much she went over it in her head, it wouldn't change a thing. It was done and she'd have to live with the consequences of her choices. That little fact made her grit her teeth together in annoyance.

If only she could have gone back in time and warned herself how messy this would get.

Men, she cursed as she tossed and turned between the sheets. *Fucking useless men. Can't handle a woman who knows what she wants.*

Kate rolled onto her side, fluffed up the pillow beneath her head, and tried to get comfortable. Soon enough her anger faded, allowing her to drift off into a dreamless, easy sleep.

The next morning, she awoke to the sunlight pouring through her windows. For a split second, Kate managed to forget about her troubles. It didn't last long, though. Thoughts pounded in her mind, reminding her of the stupid choices she'd made.

Kate wasn't going to sulk about it, though. She got up out of bed and got changed, wearing her trusty bikini beneath her loose-fitting clothes. She wasn't going to let one man ruin her vacation. She came here to unwind and that was exactly what she was going to do, no matter what.

She went down into the lobby, on her way to the beach, when she saw a small table set up off in one corner, hidden out of sight. Kate walked up to it as her eyes drifted up and down the little display they had next to the table. It was a place to book tours and sightseeing in the local area.

Kate drifted up to the table and saw a bus tour. It was at least ten hours long, taking them all around the nearby cities and through the countryside. Kate knew that she'd be able to see so many beautiful landscapes while, at the same time, getting away from Gerard for a day.

Without really thinking, she booked herself a tour for the next day. She was informed she would have to be ready bright and early at seven the next morning. Kate felt her heart flutter with excitement as she thought about getting away from the hotel.

The day passed in an easy, sandy blur. After spending most of her day at the far corner of the beach, soaking up the sun and getting a great tan going, she headed back up to her hotel room for a peaceful night's sleep.

When her alarm went off at six-thirty, Kate almost leaped out of bed, ready to start the day. She got ready as quickly as she could, covering her body in white, tight, comfortable clothes, and went straight down to the lobby.

People were already hanging around by the front doors as workers prepared the bus. Most of the people were couples, holding hands or leaning their heads on each other's shoulders as they waited. Kate stayed at the back of the group, feeling a little out of place.

She was in a beautiful country, in a beautiful hotel, surrounded by couples on their honeymoons. It was clear to her that she might have been better off at a cheaper hotel that was more party-oriented. That way she might have found men willing for lust-fueled one-night-stands.

There was nothing she could do about it now, though. She was here and she knew she had to make the most of it.

What else was she going to do? She couldn't switch hotels and she certainly couldn't go home. What was there for her? A daughter that didn't need her and a job that was looking for a way to fire her.

Sighing, Kate let her eyes drift forward as she watched the men preparing the van. They were cleaning out trash, most likely from the previous day's tour. With their clear little bags and black gloves, the men worked tirelessly to make the bus clean for them.

It didn't take long for the bus to fill up. Kate hung back, not eager to pile into a bus filled with happy couples. She waited at the back of the line and made her way slowly onto the bus. Luckily there was a double set of seats free so she could sit all by herself.

Kate sat next to the window and placed her purse on the seat beside her, preventing anyone from sitting there. People were still coming, rushing to the bus as they laughed and joked with their loved ones.

Kate ignored them all as she waited for the bus to just hurry up and move already. A quick glance at her cell phone told her that it was almost eight in the morning. They were supposed to have left half an hour ago.

The last couple of people came onto the bus and searched through the seats to find a space. The last man walked through the center of the bus slowly, staring at each person he passed.

Kate tried not to pay too much attention to him but he looked so familiar. She must have seen him somewhere else in the hotel, with his striking brown eyes and jet black hair smoothed back from his face.

When his eyes connected with hers, a wide smile burst over his lips, revealing his perfectly white teeth. Kate couldn't rip her eyes away from his face as he smiled and walked up to the seat next to her.

He looked down to the spot, where her purse was taking up the seat, and nodded to it.

"Do you mind?" He asked, his thickly accented voice rolling through the whole bus.

Kate grabbed her purse and brought it into her lap, holding it against her chest as the man sat down next to her. When she glanced over to the side of his face, a memory flashed behind her eyes.

Standing at the elevator, flirting with him, smiling coyly as she looked into his deep brown eyes and enjoyed the look of his slick, jet-black hair.

A burst of electric energy rattled around Kate's stomach. She tried not to make her attraction obvious but constantly giving the man side-eyed glances wasn't exactly sly.

It didn't take him long to pick up on her curiosity and turned in the seat, his smile stretching over his teeth.

"I know you," he said slowly, his accent thick and heavy, "don't I?"

Kate nodded, trying not to grin like an idiot. "Yes," she said. "We met outside the elevator in the hotel."

The man frowned, bringing his dark eyebrows together. "Mmm," he sighed. "I think I remember you falling into my arms?"

"That was me," Kate said, feeling herself start to blush.

She couldn't remember the last time a man had made her feel this way. Excited, nervous, even a little bit shy. Everything about him exuded confidence. The way he talked, the way he held himself in the seat, just the air around him.

It was intoxicating. Kate knew that it would be a bad idea to take this guy to bed. How much more trouble could she get herself in? But as her eyes drifted up and down his perfectly sculpted body, his muscles bulging even beneath his thick shirt, she couldn't help but imagine letting her tongue run all over his skin.

Maybe I don't have to take him to bed, she thought. *Maybe we can go somewhere else.*

Kate continued to eye fuck him without thinking twice about it. He was busy looking through the bus, waiting for the tour to start, not paying any attention to her.

That was fine with Kate. She was free to look at every inch of his face and his body as much as she liked. She could feel the saliva rushing into her mouth as if she were looking at a tasty snack. Her eyes drifted over his pecs, his abs, his arms. Everything she saw was perfection.

When the tour began, Kate was overly pleased that he leaned into her space to look out of their shared window. She was instantly intoxicated by his smell, a musty fragrance that floated up her nose and straight into her brain.

By the time the bus stopped, Kate felt like she had fallen into a frenzied dream. All she could think about was tearing off this man's clothes and she didn't even know his name yet.

People began to pile out slowly, bumping into one another as they hustled. Kate was confused. She hadn't heard anyone say anything about a stop just yet but she had been too busy ogling the man beside her to know much of anything.

As everyone started to leave, Kate saw that he was staring at her. She looked into his brown eyes and frowned a little.

"May I ask your name?" He asked, a crooked smile edging onto his lips.

"Kate," she answered instantly.

The man held out his hand for her to shake. "Marcus," he said, rolling the *r*-sound. "Pleased to meet you."

Kate shook his hand and smiled. "Likewise."

A weight lifted off her shoulders now that she knew his name. He kept staring into her eyes as he rose from the seat, his head craning down to look at her. His smile never faltered.

"What's going on?" Kate asked, watching as he collected his belongings.

"Lunch break," he said. "You didn't hear them announce it?"

Kate shrugged and shook her head. "Guess not."

"Hm," Marcus smiled knowingly. "I suppose it's hard to concentrate when staring at a man's chest."

*

Kate felt her stomach drop through her body as the words circled around her head, bouncing off the inside of her skull. She could feel the blood rushing into her cheeks, causing her to flush, but luckily Marcus's back was already turned to her.

He'd thrown his messenger bag over his shoulder and was walking down the aisle of the bus. Kate could see him smiling as he made his way out into the fresh air.

There was nothing else for her to do but climb off the bus herself. She was the last person on board. Everyone else could be seen outside the windows, stretching their legs and arms as they moved in front of the small cafe.

As Kate stepped outside, she realized that they were on top of a huge, grassy hill. A few trees were dotted around, but the most beautiful thing was the rolling landscape around her. Not all of it was covered in grass, but the land spread out in front of her for miles. The sun was beating down on her from above, lighting the entire world ahead of her.

She could hear people talking and laughing as they ordered their lunch. Kate considered joining in with the group to try and fit in, but she wasn't hungry. Not for food, anyway.

A body stood a couple of feet away from her, the sound of the shoes crunching against the gravel. Kate looked over her shoulder to see Marcus there, a smirk on his lips.

"Beautiful, isn't it?" He asked.

"Not the most beautiful thing I've seen all day," Kate agreed. "But, still, it's pretty good."

Marcus raised his thick, black eyebrow as he stared down at her. Then his smirk broke out into a grin. Without missing a beat, he held out his hand for Kate to take. It was as if he'd read her mind.

Maybe she wasn't as smooth as she thought she was, but she didn't care. She grabbed hold of his hand and allowed him to lead her away from the group. He didn't take her far, just a little way down the hill, but he made sure that they weren't visible from above.

As soon as they were safe, Marcus put his hands on the back of Kate's neck and pulled her in for a kiss. He smashed his lips against hers and yanked her body against his, keeping her tight in his grasp. Kate couldn't stop the moan from vibrating through her throat as Marcus slipped his tongue into her mouth.

Her stomach roiled. Butterflies flapped their wings inside of her. A hot wave rolled through her body, sending shivers and tingles up and down her spine.

He wasn't what she usually went for, but she supposed that the vacation was a good time to explore. After all, she hardly ever had such a stunning man eagerly kissing her after knowing her for less than a couple of hours. Another little experiment couldn't hurt, especially considering the previous fiasco.

Marcus's strong hand made its way down to the small of her back, pressing her pelvis against his as his finger dug into the back of her neck. Kate wrapped her arms around his neck, pulling him down to her ferociously.

Within a couple of seconds, they were rolling around on the grass, their legs entangled with each other's as they continued to kiss. Kate felt her head and back knock against the hard ground but she didn't care. She followed his lips, even if that meant they would roll over and over in an endless loop.

They stopped rolling for long enough and Marcus moved his hands away from Kate's waist to rip off her clothes. She could barely feel his hands on her body. The only thing she was aware of was his lips on hers, and the pressure of his body on top of her.

She didn't care that he was making all of the moves. She didn't care that he was on top. She didn't even care that he held all the power. All she could think about was how wet she was, how hot he was, and how much she wanted to feel his cock inside of her.

Kate felt him pull off her pants and spread her legs with his rough, warm hands. She looked up to him, deep into his brown eyes, and rocked her head up to whisper in his ear.

"Fuck me," she whispered, her voice trembling. "Fuck me hard."

Marcus didn't need to be told twice. He pulled out his huge erection and barely gave Kate a second to look at it. He put his head between her lower lips and pushed himself inside.

There wasn't any need to go easy. He kept on pushing his cock inside her, allowing gentle groans to come out of his open mouth. Kate couldn't hold herself back, either. A loud groan rumbled from her throat and traveled through the air quickly.

In reply, Marcus slapped his hand over her mouth. He pressed his lips against her neck and let his teeth bite at the skin there. Kate felt her body shiver at the sensation and another moan burst out of her. At least that time it was muffled.

When Marcus's pelvis was tight against hers, he removed his hand from her mouth and instead grabbed her hands and raised them above her head. He held them there with one hand and embedded his other hand into the dirt.

With his head angled down, he began to pull his cock out of her. Kate couldn't help but look down, too. They both watched as his enormous, veiny cock slipped in and out of her pussy slowly.

Both of them moaned and hissed through their teeth but were careful to keep the noises to the minimum. The group was just above them, at the top of the hill, eating their lunch. Just because Kate and Marcus were animals, it didn't mean everyone else was. They had to keep quiet.

Kate felt her muscles tightening as she stared down at Marcus's cock. His pelvis was hitting against her clitoris, rubbing her in all the right ways. Marcus looked up to her, seemingly able to feel her intense arousal, and let his hands slip away from her wrists.

He reached down between their legs and pressed his four fingers against her clitoris. He rummaged around, picking up her wetness on his fingers, before finally starting to rub her clitoris.

Instantly Kate felt her body react. Her pussy clenched around his cock as a hot orgasm rolled through her body, causing all of her muscles to clamp down and release in a strong, hypnotic rhythm.

Marcus tried to hold in his moans just as much as Kate. The only way he could do that was by kissing her, letting his tongue invade her mouth once more. He continued to pound her as his fingers worked on her, bringing her closer to orgasm once more.

Kate could feel the sweat on her forehead and the pounding, aching heartbeat inside her chest. She felt his cock sliding in and out of her, pressing and stretching her insides with its girth. It was hard to stifle herself, but she had to.

She could feel another orgasm coming, rising inside her body like a burning heat. She could feel her muscles start to clench, then her breaths turned ragged, and then it hit. A wave of heat and sweat and euphoria, all of it pulsing through her body as she bit down on her bottom lip.

Above her, Marcus's body shuddered. A long groan came out of his mouth and within a split second his cock throbbed. Kate felt his semen filling her up as he came, spurting up inside her, warm and wet.

Both of them were panting, covered in sweat and grass, with huge smiles on their lips. Marcus pulled his cock out of her and rolled onto his back. Kate looked over at him, watching his chest rise and fall.

"That was great," she said, breathing heavily between the words. "Thanks."

"No, thank you," Marcus purred.

Kate sat up on the grass and reached for her pants. As soon as she moved, she could feel Marcus's seed coming out of her. She grimaced at the feeling and, for a second, thought that it might have been a bad idea to fuck a random on a bus tour. She was going to have to sit in his cum for hours.

Still, there was nothing she could do about that now. She put on her pants and checked her body over, making sure that everything was in order before standing up.

When she did, Marcus leaned his head up and shaded his eyes. "Where you going?" He asked, grabbing for her ankle.

"Gotta use the restroom," Kate said, sidestepping his outstretched hand. "You might want to put your cock away."

She walked up the hill, listening to the sound of Marcus cursing and the rustling of his jeans, and couldn't help but let a huge smile spread across her face.

Eyes instantly moved to her face. Kate saw their mouths moving, the edges of their lips pulled down. Some of them were frowning at her, shaking their heads.

Kate continued on walking, making her way to the restroom she'd seen on the side of the cafe. She didn't care about those old dried-up hags and judgmental men. Their opinions meant nothing to her.

She let their looks and stares wash off her back like water on a duck's feathers, but it didn't stop the feeling of eyes boring into her back.

She wanted to turn her head and stare them down, maybe give them the finger, but the last thing she needed was to be kicked off the tour and left stranded in the middle of nowhere.

There was a queue ahead of her. A couple of old, fat women with ugly straw hats balanced on their heads. When they saw her coming, they turned their backs and whispered to each other.

Kate allowed herself to roll her eyes then. Of course they were old American women from the south, and of course, they were judging her. No doubt they'd spied her running down the hill with Marcus and it had insulted their gentle Christian dispositions.

It made no difference to her. Kate didn't care if they labeled her a slut, a whore, or a dirty woman. Those were labels she'd wear with pride. Shaming women for their natural sexuality was something that disgusted her. It was a barrier she was willing to break.

When it was her turn to enter the restroom, Kate immediately washed her hands in the sink. She was going to have to do some serious clean-up down there and she didn't need dirty bits of grass getting stuck in her most gentle of areas.

With her hands sparkling clean, Kate moved to the right to dry her hands with some paper towels and caught a glimpse of herself in the mirror. A hoarse laugh burst out of her mouth.

She was covered in grass stains. Her face, her neck, even her damn hair. Not only that, but she had blades of grass and small twigs tangled in the mop of bird's nest hair on her head.

Kate pressed her lips together, trying to keep her laughter quiet, as she pried out the grass and twigs and tried to untangle the knots. Those women might have been judging her for having carefree sex in public, but they were probably more shocked by the way she looked.

It was so very clear what she'd been doing at the bottom of that hill. No wonder those old ladies looked so offended by her mere presence. Kate giggled to herself, feeling like a naughty schoolgirl, as she fixed herself up.

Chapter Twelve

Voracious

KATE WAS ONE OF the first people to clamber out of the bus. The more time she spent sitting next to Marcus, the more she realized that he just wasn't for her. She didn't want to be trapped next to him for a moment longer.

Unfortunately for her, Marcus was incredibly eager. He followed her out of the bus, pushing and shoving his way through the crowd, and grabbed her elbow. Kate spun around to face him, surprised by his forcefulness.

"Where are you running off to?" Marcus asked, laughing. "I want to spend some more time with you."

Kate gracefully pried her elbow out of Marcus's grasp and clutched onto the strap of her purse, trying to protect herself from his advances. Despite the fact that she'd just had sex with him—in public, no less—she just didn't want anything more to do with him.

"I'm sorry," Kate said, forcing a fake smile onto her lips. "I'm exhausted. I'm going back up to my room to have a nap."

Marcus raised his eyebrow, smirking at her. "A nap?" he asked. "I'll join you."

Kate frowned, shocked at how pushy he was being. "No," she insisted. "You won't be joining me."

"Why not?" Marcus asked. "Are you done with me now?"

Kate resisted the urge to roll her eyes. "Look," she sighed. "I'm just here to have some fun, okay? I work hard and I deserve this vacation. So, I'm going to go upstairs and have a nap on my own. That doesn't mean anything. It just means I want some time alone to decompress from the very strange day I've had."

Marcus nodded slowly, seeming as though he was understanding what Kate was trying to say.

"Great," she said, allowing herself to smile for real. "That's great. Thanks for today. It was fun."

Just as Kate turned around, heading toward the elevators, Marcus grabbed her elbow again. Kate gritted her teeth together as she turned back around toward him. She could feel the anger rising up in her chest, threatening to burst out of her mouth in a brutal barrage.

"Yes?" Kate asked, trying to keep her voice steady.

"Can I take you to dinner later?" Marcus asked, completely ignorant of her anger. "Outside of the hotel? To a nice place. Maybe sushi?"

Kate sighed and looked down at her shoes, shaking her head slowly.

"Come on," Marcus moaned. "You can't just entice me in by fucking me then deny me your time."

Kate looked up into his eyes, suddenly serious. "I absolutely can," she snapped. "I don't owe you anything."

Marcus shifted his weight from foot to foot as he sighed. "I didn't mean it like that," he said. "I just want to get to know you better."

"Maybe I don't," Kate shrugged. "Maybe I just want to go upstairs, have a nap, and be left alone."

Marcus's face fell as he stared at her, digesting her words. He let go of her elbow and Kate took the opportunity to rush off. She wasn't in the mood to be grabbed and pulled around.

When she got up into her hotel room, she locked the door behind her and put the safety chain across the door, just to be safe.

Only then did she allow herself to relax. Her shoulders slumped as she let her neck go loose. She leaned her head forward and rubbed the back of her neck, trying to knead out the stress from her muscles.

She made her way to the bed and perched on the edge, still trying to release the tension from her neck. While sitting there, she looked out the glass door to the little balcony outside her room.

It was dark out there with a breeze blowing through the trees surrounding the beach. She could barely see the sand or the waves, but she knew it was out there.

As she sat there, she wondered why all men were so crazy. She hadn't been able to have carefree, emotionless sex so far on this trip. Back when she was younger, that was all men seemed to want. Now that she was older, it felt like men had changed their ways when she wasn't paying attention.

It was true, she hadn't been with someone in a very long time. She'd been so busy getting divorced from her husband, working hard in her career, and raising her daughter that she hadn't had time to date.

Had all of the men just turned their backs on their slutty ways? Kate hoped not. She was counting on them to come through for her on this vacation. That was what she needed the most—lots of lovers before she had to go back to the daily grind of her old life.

Kate didn't want to sit and ruminate on it any longer. She curled up in the middle of her huge bed and closed her eyes, wishing for sleep. She tossed and turned for a while, unable to stop her mind from turning.

All she could think about was her ex-husband. He'd been an absolute ass to her. He'd turned his back on their family and left them to fend for themselves.

It wasn't surprising that Kate had issues after that. Why would she want to get close to another man when they treated her like that? No, it was easier to use and abuse them, and then set them free into the wild.

That wasn't working for her, though. No matter what she did, the men came running after her like lost puppies. Their eyes were all big and round as they begged her to *please, please miss, please keep me for yourself.*

Kate was almost disgusted by their behavior. It was pathetic and it certainly wasn't sexy. As soon as men turned into those soft, sappy masses, Kate knew it was her time to leave.

Before this vacation, she hadn't had time to have a man in her life. Now that she had time, she wondered if it was all it was cracked up to be. All those years she spent without a man between her legs. It hadn't been so bad, and she hadn't had to deal with all of this drama.

Then it dawned on her. For twelve years, she hadn't had sex. Kate sat up in her bed, staring at nothing in particular, as she did the math.

Was it really twelve years? Kate thought.

She got up from the bed and began to pace as she counted. There had been dates, dancing, and dinners. But none of them had gone any further. She'd always come home alone to her big house.

Kate let her hand come up to her lips, picking at the cracked skin there, as she continued to worry about the fact that she had spent a huge portion of her life without a good dicking.

This was unbelievable to her. She'd never calculated how long it had been or realized how much of life she'd been missing out on. Sure, these men that she had chosen on vacation, they weren't the best of the best, but she knew there were men out there just like her. They existed. She just had to find them.

Kate knew that she couldn't stay in her hotel room tonight. She had to make up for all that lost time. She'd had orgasms, sure. She'd watched her fair share of porn and used her dildos and vibrators to please herself, but was it the same as having a living, breathing body between her legs?

No, was the only word going through her mind. No, it wasn't the same. No, it wasn't good enough. No, she wasn't going to stay in this hotel room all night and waste the precious time she had left.

She needed to make the most of this vacation and lazing around wasn't the way to do it. Kate rushed to the dresser and began to search through it, looking for something sexy for her to wear.

When she'd roamed the streets outside the hotel, she'd seen so many different bars and clubs and cafes. One of them had to be open. One of them had to have enough men in there to whet her appetite.

Kate kept reminding herself that she'd had two bad experiences with men already. She wasn't about to have another one tonight. Sure, the sex had been good enough for her, but it wasn't what she was looking for.

Passion, heat, steam. That's what she was looking for. And none of the previous fucks had been able to provide that. Marcus was close, but he was too macho for her. Kate liked to take control... and that's exactly what she was going to do.

Chapter Thirteen

Three or nothing

Kate felt the darkness around her. It was almost stifling, clinging to her body and surrounding her. Pulsing neon lights shot down to the floor in all shapes and colors as she danced in the middle of the room.

There were bodies all around her, knocking into her as they jumped and danced, but she didn't care. The music was throbbing through her body, the bass taking over her bones and vibrating them into oblivion.

Her hands roamed up and down her body as she swayed beneath the bright lights. Her hips popped from side to side as her hands went up into her hair, grabbing fistfuls of it as she turned and twirled.

Somehow, she had forgotten about her troubles and had let the music take over. With only a couple of drinks inside of her, Kate felt freer than she had in a long time.

All she wanted to do was dance and drink and fuck the night away. That's exactly what she was going to do. There was plenty of time left on the clock and there were more than enough men.

A couple of them had been eyeing her as she danced. Kate had been watching them coyly, making sure to try to entice them with her fit, toned body.

The dress she was wearing was skimpy at best. It had spaghetti straps that barely held up the thin material over her breasts. It was a dark beige color, matching her skin tone perfectly. At first glance, it looked like she was naked.

Kate always felt sexy in that dress. Men's eyes were always on her, feeding her already-inflated ego. Sweat dripped down her back as she worked her body, droplets dripping down with the curve of her spine.

It didn't matter to her, though. All she cared about was having fun. She felt her body moving to the beat around her, her muscles finally getting that sweet release that they so desperately needed.

She could feel eyes on her, eyes from every corner of the room, but Kate didn't pay them any attention. She knew she could have her pick so she wasn't going to go home with the first man she saw—she was going to take her time, find one that would be willing to submit to her whims.

This vacation was eye-opening for her. For the last twelve years of her life, she hadn't had a second thought about men. They hadn't starred in her life. They just weren't important.

For whatever reason, now she felt that they were. She needed to get out there and enjoy herself before she dried up. Sure, watching porn was hot and it did the job, but did it compare to connecting with another person? Looking them in the eye while their bodies were intertwined?

Kate obviously thought that wasn't important at all in the past, but now she wasn't so sure. All she could do was dance and hope that she attracted someone who was sexually compatible.

Her arms grew tired and shaky, as did her legs. She knew she needed a break, so she wobbled over to the bar to sit down and have a drink. She wasn't twenty-one anymore—her days of dancing the night away were long behind her, clearly.

As she sipped her vodka on the rocks, she looked around the dim bar, trying to spot an attractive man that she could possibly take home. There were several macho, alpha men eyeing her but she knew they wouldn't work. They would want to take control and they certainly wouldn't let Kate defile their bodies like she wanted to.

With her elbows on the bar behind her and her chest pushed out, she stared over the dance floor. Men and women were grinding on each other, sweating into their clothes as they whipped their heads and hips.

It was intoxicating just watching them, smelling them, feeling the music roll through her body. The longer Kate stayed in the club, the more she felt herself getting turned on.

There were so many beautiful bodies. So many men to have her way with. She considered taking one to the restroom and fucking his brains out just so she could clear her head, but she knew that wasn't a good idea.

She'd already had two misadventures since arriving here. She didn't want another one. The second fuck with Gerard was fantastic, but the look in his eyes would haunt her. He looked so betrayed and horrified. How could she do that to someone else?

There was no question about it. She had to find someone willing and able to do what she needed. It would make her life a little harder, and a little more complicated, but it would be worth it.

Around the club, she could see several candidates—men that were eyeing her up but were clearly too shy to come up to her and ask her for a dance.

The largest man had arms as big as her head, a huge chest, and a slim waist. His body was sculpted to perfection and it was clearly something he was proud of, since he wore an impossibly tight shirt to show off all those bulging, throbbing muscles.

Just looking at him got Kate wet. What a perfect image of masculinity he was. And yet, he was too afraid to come and talk to Kate. She could see him adoring every inch of her body, it was obvious, but he still wouldn't come over.

Maybe he won't, Kate thought. *He has an imposing figure. Maybe he doesn't want to scare women away by lumbering over to them.*

Kate thought he would be an easy target, anyway. The women were flocking around him. Some of them looked at least a decade younger than herself. She didn't need competition tonight.

Her eyes gazed around the club more, looking for eyes on hers, trying to see through the dim light and moving bodies. Finally, she saw two men at the end of the bar. Both of them looked young, young enough to be her sons, but that didn't bother Kate.

She downed the rest of her drink as she sized them up. The boy on the left had a sweet, round face. Everything about him looked soft. His shoulders were rounded and his stomach looked a little full, clearly from drinking too much of that beer he was swigging.

The boy to the right, though, he was the polar opposite. His body was small but firm and he was dressed in a tight tank top to show off his hard work. Of course, the muscles were nothing compared to old barrel chest across the dance floor, but Kate wasn't into pissing contests.

Both of them looked cute and shy. They only made themselves look younger as they began to bicker amongst each other as they stared over at her. Clearly, they are arguing over who was coming over to talk to her.

Kate smirked and decided to make the decision easier for them. She set her empty glass on the bar and slipped off the stool. Out of the corner of her eye, she could see both boys grab onto one another as their mouths popped open.

They stayed there for a second, completely shocked that Kate had the audacity to move while they were fighting over her, before scrambling into movement. They shoved their arms into each other as they tried to slip off the stools as well.

Kate wanted to roll her eyes at their severe childishness but it didn't matter. They wouldn't be behaving childishly for long, not if she had her way.

She swayed her hips as she walked toward them, making sure to look through her eyelashes and make eye contact with both the boys. They stopped, stock-still, as they gawked at her approaching.

When Kate was within touching distance, she reached out and squeezed both of their upper arms.

"Let me buy you boys a drink," she said, straining her voice to be heard over the pulsing music.

Both of them tittered and laughed as they sat back down into their seats, clearly unable to believe their luck. Kate raised her arm over their heads and motioned at the bartender for two more drinks.

When she was sitting down beside them with her vodka in hand, she started trying to get all the information out of them that she needed. They were twenty-six and twenty-nine, with the pudgier of the two being the younger. The older man was Alessandro, here from Spain with his best friend, Fabian.

Kate couldn't help but be a little disappointed. She wanted them both and she knew that these self-proclaimed best friends were unlikely to go with it. Men got so testy being naked around other men they knew well.

"You boys are very cute," Kate said, smiling as widely as she could as she nibbled on the straw dunked into her drink. "So very cute."

"As are you," Fabian said quickly.

"I'd say sexy," Alessandro added.

"So very sexy," Fabian agreed.

Both of them were leaning forward in their seats, edging as close to her as they could get. It was a good sign. Kate could basically see them starting to drool over her.

"How about we go somewhere more private?" she asked. "Just us three?"

The boys broke out into a deep grin before realizing what she was saying. They glanced at one another, their smiles fading.

"Both of us?" Fabian asked. "Alessandro too?"

"That's what three means," Kate smirked. "You, and me, and Alessandro."

Their eyes bulged out of their sockets. They looked between each other, their dark, oiled hair glistening in the neon lights above. They weren't going to go for it. Kate felt the disappointment wash through her like the ocean, cold and biting.

She ignored them as they spoke amongst themselves, suddenly feeling bored and rejected. That wasn't a way that Kate liked to feel. She'd chosen them out of everyone else in the bar and they were going to turn her down.

A challenge, Kate thought. *I should make it a challenge.*

As she sat there, she tried to figure out how to convince these boys to come with her. If she said she just wanted to talk to them, to get to know them better, then they might agree. Once she had them out of the club and somewhere private, she could convince them in... other ways.

Kate touched each of their arms, gently caressing their skin, grabbing their attention immediately. They stopped talking and looked to her, their eyes wide and eager.

"I just want to talk," Kate purred at them. "Get to know you better. That's all."

Somehow, the words worked like magic on the boys. Within a second they were eager to follow her out of the club. Kate may as well have been a big, shiny lure dumped into the middle of a big lake. They followed her so willingly it was almost laughable.

Outside, the air was cool against all of Kate's bare skin. She instantly felt all the sweat on her body turn cold, sending shivers through her body. It felt nice compared to the stifling, sweaty heat indoors.

When the boys were outside behind her, she linked arms with them and began to walk with them, heading toward the hotel. Neither of them seemed to mind her taking the lead. It was a good sign.

"So," Kate smirked. "I like you boys. A lot. And I think it would be great if you'd come back to my hotel room for some much-needed fun."

Fabian tensed up. "What kind of fun?"

"You know what fun I mean," Kate laughed. "The naked kind."

"Listen, lady," Fabian started.

Alessandro immediately dropped Kate's arm and grabbed Fabian's collar before yanking him away. Alessandro draped his arm over Fabian's shoulder as he talked to him excitedly in their native Spanish.

Kate had never taken Spanish at school and had no idea what they were saying. She knew the gist of it, though. Alessandro wanted this—Fabian didn't.

"No!" Fabian shouted, before shrugging Alessandro's arm off his shoulder. "No, never."

Alessandro turned around to look at Kate, a pained expression on his face.

"What's the matter?" Kate asked, her voice as soft as silk. "Your friend doesn't like me?"

"No, no, no, no, no," Alessandro said, elongating the *oh*-sound on the last word. "It's not like that. He just doesn't want to... be in the same room as me."

"One at a time?" Kate asked.

Both of the boys nodded enthusiastically. "Yes," Fabian said. "That I will be okay with."

Kate shook her head and shrugged. "Sorry," she said. "It's either both of you at the same time, or nothing at all."

Fabian started shouting in Spanish almost instantly. Alessandro turned to his friend, desperate to convince him to agree, but Fabian wasn't having any of it.

As much as Kate enjoyed ruining friendships, this wasn't why she was here. She needed some cock between her legs. Watching these two fight was turning her drier than the Sahara desert.

"All right," Kate sighed. "I'm going back to my hotel room now. You missed your chance."

Without looking back at them, she turned on her heels and began walking back. She could feel her shoes pinching her feet and the air was whipping against her thighs, stinging her skin.

The alcohol was wearing off and her libido was sinking. All she wanted was some casual sex with two beautiful men, but apparently that was too much to ask for.

Kate could feel the disappointment radiating out of her as she hung her head. Behind her, she could still hear the boys arguing. She tried to tell herself that they were the ones missing out but she didn't quite believe it.

Chapter Fourteen

How much do you want it?

THE STARS ABOVE HER glinted, most of them hiding behind the thin dusting of clouds. Kate looked up to them as she wobbled back to her hotel room, thinking about all the possibilities that were lost.

The boys that she'd wanted to take back to the hotel were long behind her, still arguing. She could hear their voices rolling through the air, snippets of their Spanish floating into her ears.

None of it made any sense to her but she knew what they were arguing about: her. Alessandro's thick, heavy voice was only getting louder and louder whereas Fabian's gentle voice was barely audible.

It wasn't any of Kate's business, anyway. She tried to block the sounds out as she trundled back. Her shoulders felt heavy and her back was slumped with disappointment.

All of her dreams were shattered. When she'd seen those boys eyeing her up, she imagined all the fun she could have had with them. Two bodies, two cocks, two mouths. The possibilities were limitless.

Stop thinking about it, Kate thought. *You'll just get yourself worked up over it. What's the point?*

"Kate!" she heard a voice scream. "Kaaaate!"

She turned around just in time to see Alessandro sprinting toward her with his left hand raised above his head, waving manically to get her attention.

A smirk burst onto her lips as she watched his ridiculous run. He was desperate to have her, that much was clear. She stopped walking and waited for him to catch up to her. He stopped short of her and bent over, pressing his palms into his knees as he panted deeply.

"Kate," he breathed, still facing the floor. "Kate. Fabian agreed."

Her heart started to race in her chest. "He did?"

"Yes," Alessandro wheezed. "Yes, he wants to. He wants to."

Kate looked behind Alessandro and saw Fabian walking slowly toward her. It seemed to be true. She had two willing boys, throwing themselves at her mercy. Her smirk turned into a grin.

"That's fantastic," she purred. "Come with me."

And then she held out her hand for Alessandro to take. He grabbed it and held it tightly, so eager to get going. They waited for Fabian to catch up and when Kate held out her hand for him, he reluctantly took it.

She knew that this wasn't going to be a good time for him if she couldn't show him that tonight would be worth his while. Kate stopped walking and dropped both the men's hands.

"You're not into this," she said to Fabian.

His eyes instantly looked over to Alessandro, wide and apologetic. Kate didn't care, though. She just sank down to her knees and let her fingers pry open his jeans.

Fabian gasped and tried to stop her hands but Kate continued. Within a second she had his cock in her hand, pumping it gently. Fabian groaned and tried to cover himself with both of his hands.

"Stop looking," he complained to Alessandro. "Stop!"

Alessandro tittered and turned his back, shaking his head as he looked down to the ground. Kate ignored them both and continued working on Fabian.

"Just relax," she cooed. "Relax. That's it."

She felt his cock start to pulse as blood rushed into it. After a couple of seconds, it had already grown an inch and it showed no signs of stopping.

Fabian threw his head back and started to breathe heavily as Kate continued to touch him lovingly. He was growing in her palm so quickly that it was almost too much to handle.

Kate wasn't going to waste any more time. She needed to show him that she was serious about this. She opened her mouth and eased his cock inside, making sure to lap her tongue against his skin, getting it slick with her saliva.

Fabian gasped loudly, followed by a throaty moan. Kate felt his body shift as he looked down at her.

"Oh my god," he whispered.

Kate suppressed a smile as she took his cock farther into her mouth. She could taste his salty, sweaty skin against her tongue. The feeling of his hard cock inside of her turned her on, causing her pussy to clench and drip into her underwear.

"Woah," Alessandro said, looking over his shoulder at what Kate was doing.

"Shut up, man," Fabian groaned.

"Jesus Christ," Alessandro cried. "She's going *at it*!"

"Shut up," Fabian hissed. "I'm trying to concentrate."

"Dude, you're doin' it wrong," Alessandro laughed. "The whole point is not to concentrate."

"Shut up," Fabian moaned. "I'm losing it."

Alessandro turned around and folded his arms across his chest. Kate couldn't help but smirk as she worked on Fabian. These boys were so inexperienced, it was laughable.

It didn't matter. Once the evening was done, they'd know a lot more. Then she'd set them free into the wild, a gift to all the other women they came across.

When Fabian's cock had recovered from the distraction, Kate decided to take this a step further. She took his cock right to the back of her mouth, slipping down her throat.

The only thing Fabian could do was gasp and clutch onto the back of her head, basically moaning as she sucked his cock. Having so much power over him was like crack to her. She could feel her whole body vibrating with sexual energy as she opened her mouth wider and took him deeper.

Her knees were sore against the darkened sidewalk but she didn't care. The only thing that mattered to her was the tension in her stomach and the hot, pulsing feeling in her pussy. She was dripping, so ready to have their cocks inside her, but she knew she had to do more convincing.

Fabian's body started to twitch as he grew closer to orgasm. Kate knew it was her time to switch. The last thing she wanted was for Fabian to blow his load before she was ready.

Kate reached out and grabbed hold of Alessandro's crotch. He turned around instantly, silently looking down at her in shock. Kate removed her mouth from around Fabian's cock and looked up to Alessandro, feeling the fire burning in her eyes.

Wordlessly, she pulled Alessandro's cock out of his pants and began to work on him, her hand tight around his member. It took him much less time to get hard. His dick grew like magic, eagerly awaiting her mouth with a drop of precum on the head.

Kate took him into her mouth gladly, tasting his arousal on her tongue. It was salty but sweet, a pleasant taste that she never seemed to tire of.

As she sucked him, taking his cock deeper into her mouth, she heard Alessandro start to moan.

It was a gentle, sweet sound, unlike his usual personality. Unlike Fabian, he didn't care if anyone saw. He was wholly in the moment, enjoying the feeling of his dick getting sucked.

Kate could feel her neck getting tense and sore from all the bobbing but she was determined to convince them that she meant business. She sucked Alessandro hard, wrapping her tongue around his cock as she moved her head back and forth.

He groaned louder and more confidently as he grabbed the back of Kate's head, helping her along in giving him a blowjob. She continued until she felt him getting too excited, his whole body tensing as the orgasm started to come.

She detached his hands from the back of her head and removed his cock from her mouth, leaving him gasping and moaning as the cold air rushed around his member.

Without looking back at him, she turned straight for Fabian and was pleasantly surprised to see him pumping his own cock, staying erect as he watched her blowing Alessandro.

Kate felt her eyebrow rise up her forehead as she looked at him but she didn't say anything. It was clear he was enjoying himself, so she was going to reward him for participating.

She placed her lips around his cock and sucked harder than she'd done in a very long time. She hummed, she wrapped her lips tightly around his member, and made sure to take him all the way to the back of her throat every time she moved her head.

It only took a couple of seconds for Fabian to cum. He spurted his load all the way down the back of Kate's throat when her nose was pressed into his pelvis.

She could taste it flowing down her throat, warm and salty and sticky. Kate lessened the pressure on his cock, trying to make the experience as pleasurable as possible, before gently sucking and removing her mouth, taking all of his cum with her.

Fabian gasped as he stood there, running his hands through his hair. *Wow*, was the only thing he could manage to say as he tucked his limp erection back into his pants.

Kate looked up to Alessandro with a glint in her eyes. "Now it's your turn."

Chapter Fifteen

Top quality man-meat

KATE STOOD UP FROM the hard sidewalk and brushed off her knees as she let her lips lick the corners of her mouth. She could still taste Alessandro's cum, deep down at the back of her throat. It was sweeter than Fabian's and a little thinner, making it that much easier to go down.

Fabian had moved away from them, sitting on a nearby bench to give them some privacy, but now that Kate was back on her feet, he got up and came over to them.

Alessandro put away his cock with a huge smile on his face. "What now?"

Kate looked over at him. "Whatever you want," she said slowly. "I'm going back to my hotel room. You're free to join me if you want."

"I'm in," Alessandro blurted.

"Me too," Fabian agreed.

Kate nodded. She stepped to Fabian and grabbed his face, pulling him in for a kiss. She pressed her lips against his and lapped her tongue at his top lip, just short of going inside his mouth.

As soon as she did it, she felt Fabian's body tense up. There was no doubt in her mind that he was painfully aware of who she'd just sucked off. Kate didn't care, though. After all that hard work, she deserved a kiss.

She broke off the kiss and let Fabian's face go before turning up to Alessandro. She did the same thing, grabbing his face and kissing his lips, letting her tongue lap against his lips.

There was less resistance with Alessandro. He grabbed her hips with his hands and kissed her back savagely, shoving his tongue into her mouth. Kate broke off the kiss, gasping for breath, and smiled up at him.

I like this one, she thought. *He's up for anything.*

Now that she'd gotten her kiss from them both, she held out both of her hands to lead them back to her hotel. They both took her hand and followed her silently.

When they got up to her hotel room, both of the boys looked at her with hungry eyes. They loitered at the edge of the room with Alessandro eyeing the bed, clearly wanting to ravage her on it. Fabian was a little more laid back but equally ready.

Kate wasn't one to disappoint. She reached her fingers up to the spaghetti straps on her shoulders and hooked them down her arms.

Within a second her beige dress had fallen around her ankles in a soft lump.

Their eyes bulged out of their heads as they stared at her body. Kate held her head up high, smiling. She had nothing to be ashamed about. Her stomach was toned and muscled with barely a sign that she'd birthed a child.

Her legs were thick and sleek with no cellulite to be seen. Her breasts were perky and firm, even after all these years, and her waist was petite and grabbable.

She could see the passion in Alessandro's dark brown eyes. He was looking her whole body up and down, drinking in the sight of her. When he looked at her neatly waxed pussy, he licked his lips. That kind of eagerness was what Kate wanted to see.

Kate stepped out of the crumpled dress on the floor and moved to Alessandro, grabbing his neck with her hand. His eyes instantly locked to hers as his eyes widened, not in shock but in excitement.

Kate grabbed his crotch with her left hand, gently squeezing his package as she touched her nose against his, teasing him. Alessandro gulped, his Adam's apple grinding against the bones in her hand.

"You want me?" Kate whispered.

As soon as the words came out of her mouth, she felt Alessandro's body respond. His cock pulsed into life, starting to throb as Kate continued to apply pressure.

"Do you want me?" Kate asked, a little more forceful this time.

"Yes," Alessandro breathed. "Yes, I want you."

"Good," Kate snapped. "Then get naked."

She let go of his throat and stepped back, watching as Alessandro's shaking hands started to rip off his clothes. Kate let her eyes settle on Fabian's face, looking at him expectantly. He gulped and began to undress himself as well.

Satisfied, Kate sat on the edge of the bed and began to take off her high-heeled shoes. By the time she had them off and had tossed them to the floor, the boys were standing off to the side, completely naked.

Kate stood up from the edge of the bed and looked them up and down, sizing them up. Alessandro's body was pure perfection. His tanned skin wasn't fake or caused by the sun—it was all-natural, with every inch of his skin that beautiful golden color.

His shoulders were capped and his pecs were large and twitching. Even though he had a small frame, his muscles were impressive. Looking at his face, Kate wouldn't have been able to tell that he had such a great body. His neck was thin and his cheeks were sunken. Not the typical look of someone who clearly spent a lot of time in the gym.

Kate moved her eyes to Fabian's body. It was as she had expected—pudgy and soft, with a little beer belly starting to form. She wasn't going to judge him for it, though. He kept his pubes neat and he had ample hair on his chest, plenty for Kate to run her hands through.

They were at either end of the spectrum—average to sculpted—and she was glad she had different types of bodies to enjoy.

"Do you want me?" Kate asked Fabian.

"Y-yes," he said, nodding his head in a shaky motion.

"Then get on your knees," Kate stated.

Fabian dropped down, sending a shudder through the floor. Smiling, Kate moved in front of him, positioning her pussy right in front of his face. Fabian wasn't stupid—he knew exactly what was expected of him.

He immediately plunged his face into her trimmed bush, pressing his nose against her pelvis. Kate felt his tongue find her clitoris instantly. She couldn't stop the moan from bursting out of her mouth. It caught her off guard how quick he was at finding it and she almost lost balance.

Alessandro was there to catch her, though. He reached his arm out and grabbed hers, steadying her into place. Kate pulled him over to her and wrapped his arms around her stomach, forcing him to stand behind her.

Without prompting, Alessandro stood behind her with his growing erection pressing into her back. He leaned his head down and began to kiss the tender skin on her neck, nibbling at it and letting his heavy breaths mist on her chest.

As she stood there, the two men working on her body, Kate felt her blood soaring through her veins. She'd gotten lucky tonight, she knew that, and she was adamant that she was going to enjoy herself.

She looked down between her legs and saw Fabian looking up at her, his eyes wide as he ate her pussy, his tongue lapping at her clitoris. Then she felt his fingers at her lower lips, ready to push inside of her, but he was waiting for her permission.

Kate nodded curtly at him. Fabian closed his eyes as he shoved his tongue lower, away from her clitoris and down toward her lips, as his fingers entered her.

Her whole body rocked forward as she felt his fingers exploring her. Kate couldn't hold her head up anymore, so she leaned it back on Alessandro's chest. Her mouth popped open as Fabian continued to fuck her with his mouth, causing shudders to roll up her stomach and into her chest.

Alessandro's hands reached up from her stomach and grabbed her breasts, rolling them between his palms as his fingers made their way to her nipples. He fiddled with them, twisting them right and left, as he continued to kiss her shoulder.

Kate could barely contain herself. She felt a strong, urgent tension in her stomach as Fabian continued to lick and suck at her pussy. She was so wet down there, her lips pulsing as her blood rushed there, causing her whole body to break out into a sweat.

As her stomach started to clench, she knew she had to hold onto something. This orgasm was going to be unlike anything else. She cemented her hands onto Alessandro's sides behind her and grabbed onto him tightly.

Her breaths turned ragged as she struggled to breathe. Hot waves of ecstasy washed over her, making everything else in the world vanish. She could feel the electric spiking through her skin, making it tingle and turn to goosebumps.

Fabian moved his tongue back to her clitoris as his fingers continued to rub inside of her. There was no stopping it now, not with his warm, wet tongue lapping over her and his mouth sucking on her hard.

Kate felt a blinding heat roll through her body, starting from her pussy and rising all the way up to her head. All of the muscles in her legs and stomach clenched uncomfortably tight. It felt like all of her skin was being poked with hot needles. Every inch of her was shaking, ready to explode.

The orgasm came on strong. All of her muscles clamped down hard. Kate could barely breathe as she came, feeling like her whole body was going to shut down. Then her muscles released and euphoria pulsed through her body.

Her muscles clenched again, making it impossible for her to think of anything else, then they released. It was this over and over for a couple of seconds as the orgasm took over her whole body.

When she finally came to, the energy in the room had changed. She looked down to Fabian, whose face was still wedged between her legs, but now he was blushing.

Over her shoulder, she could feel Alessandro's chin hovering. She looked to her right and saw him staring down at his friend with a furrowed brow. It took her a moment to realize Alessandro was furiously jealous, trying to work out what the hell his friend had done to cause Kate to react that way.

As she leaned her weight against Alessandro's body, all she could think was, *good choice.*

Fabian and his magic tongue didn't waste any time. He kept on licking her, sucking her clit, moving his fingers inside of her as he searched for that elusive G-spot.

Kate's whole body felt light as if she were floating on a fluffy cloud. All these years without sex and now she was enjoying the best of the best. Not many men were this talented and Kate had somehow stumbled across him.

A shiver ran through her as Fabian's tongue plunged deeper, his nose pressing tight against her pelvis as his lips cemented themselves against her pussy. As he sucked on her slit, he shook his face from side to side, making a strange vibration roll through her bones.

Kate couldn't control herself. She threw her head back, looking up to the ceiling as she leaned on Alessandro, and let the orgasm wash over her. Every muscle in her body twitched as the hot, tingling waves reached from the tips of her toes to the top of her head.

The sweat was starting to pour off her. Breaths were coming hard and fast. She could barely keep her eyes open as she felt Fabian's mouth continue working on her, getting her ready for yet another orgasm.

She'd never had multiples like this before, so intense and absorbing. All she wanted to do was relax on the bed and let Fabian eat her all day, every day. How could she not? It was hard to resist such tantalizing pleasure.

Fabian pulled away from her, allowing a rush of cold air to surround her exposed pussy. The feeling drew Kate's attention, bringing her out of her sex coma.

She looked down at Fabian with blurry eyes.

"My jaw," he said slowly, rubbing it with his fingers.

Kate sighed and peeled herself off Alessandro's chest. "That's okay," she said slowly, making her way to the edge of the bed, her legs wobbling. "I don't think I could take much more."

Her body felt like it was giving up. Her heart was hammering and every muscle in her body felt like it was filled with battery acid. All of this just from a couple of orgasms. She couldn't believe it. She'd never been able to make herself feel like that—so how could he?

She picked up the robe on the back of the bathroom door and wrapped it around her body. Then she sat on the edge of the bed and eyed Fabian suspiciously.

"Where'd you learn how to do that?" she asked.

He shrugged as he wiped the lower portion of his face. "I don't know," he said honestly. "I do what feels right, you know?"

Kate let a strangled laugh come out of her but even laughing was too much. Her stomach was sore from all the clenching and her lungs were raw.

"I don't know," Alessandro moaned. "You need to tell me how you did that."

Kate was too tired to deal with these boys and their bullshit. She wanted to sleep after all that excitement.

A cigarette, she thought, *then a nap.*

"Either of you boys got a light?" she asked, interrupting their conversation.

Fabian instantly shoved his hand into his pocket and pulled out a pack of cigarettes and a lighter. Kate grabbed the pack and moved out to the balcony, her tired legs barely able to carry her.

The boys followed her eagerly, waiting for her to say something, anything. Kate stayed silent as she lit the cigarette and looked down at the world around them.

Below her room, the pool was covered in darkness. A few white, twinkling lights were dotted around, lighting small areas and walkways. It all looked so still out there, so calm and peaceful.

"Kate?" Alessandro asked. "Is everything okay?"

Kate looked over her shoulder at both of the boys. "Fine," she said, handing back the pack of cigarettes and lighter to Fabian. "Why don't you boys see yourselves out?"

Fabian frowned. "Did we do something wrong?"

Kate shook her head. "It's late," she said. "I'm tired. How about we do something tomorrow night? All three of us."

The boys looked between each other, a little uneasy, but they nodded eventually.

"Tomorrow," Fabian said, a sudden confidence in his voice. "We'll see you then."

Kate stayed on the balcony, puffing on her cigarette, as she watched them collect their belongings and leave her hotel room. Once the door was shut behind them, Kate relaxed on the small half-wall, giving her exhausted legs a much-needed break.

What a night, she thought. *What a hell of a night.*

Chapter Sixteen

There will be rules

THE NEXT MORNING, KATE woke with a smile on her face. It seemed that her muscles had regained some control as she sat up in bed and stretched. The morning sunshine pushed through her curtains, illuminating her room in a beautiful glow.

As she stared around at the room, she thought about how she hadn't felt this good in years. She was totally and completely relaxed. Nothing in the world could bother her, not with how she was feeling.

Kate opened her mouth and a long, silent yawn stretched her face wide open. As she breathed out, she tasted last night's cigarette on her tongue. It was bitter and her tongue felt fuzzy and gross. She went straight to the bathroom and brushed her teeth, removing the layer of gunk left behind.

Kate wanted to regret that cigarette—she'd given up the habit years ago—but last night it was definitely needed to calm her down.

When her mouth was feeling clean, she stepped out into her room and began her morning routine. She wasn't going to sit around up here when there was a whole world to explore outside. She needed more of last night, but with different men.

How could I have better men, though? she thought. *I had the best of Fabian last night. Who could get better than that?*

Kate tried not to dwell on it too much. She doubted the boys would be willing to go any further than they already did. They had been so uncomfortable with the idea of it that she was surprised she managed to convince them to go as far as they did.

Fabian was the unsure one, she reminded herself. *And when he got his lips around my pussy, he wasn't that shy anymore.*

Kate wondered if she might run into them again. She didn't want to force it and she certainly wasn't going to chase them down for another fuck. That wasn't her style.

Before she went down for breakfast, Kate glanced at the clock on the wall. The time read twelve-thirty. Kate stopped walking to stare at it, wondering if the battery had run out sometime last night. Then she saw that the second hand was moving, ticking along happily.

Frowning, Kate left her hotel room. Had she really slept the whole day away? It didn't seem likely. Kate ignored it and went downstairs, trying to stop herself from thinking of the previous night.

Of course, she couldn't stop. As she made her way to the huge dining hall, all she could think about was the sight of Fabian's lips pursed around her clit. How perfectly he'd teased her, sucked her, made her orgasm over and over and over.

The more she thought about it, the more turned on she got. She could already feel herself dripping into her underwear, soaking the material beneath her lips.

Kate tried to push the memories away as she roamed through the buffet, looking for some food to eat. Apparently, her clock had been right—everything in front of her was lunch items.

Gone were the bread rolls and fruit salads. They had been replaced with sandwiches and small salads. None of it seemed too appetizing to Kate but she knew she had to eat something.

She grabbed a small plate of salad and sat down at one of the tables, not looking forward to her meal. Why would anyone want to eat this rabbit food?

Kate rolled her eyes as she stuck her fork into a particularly crunchy piece of lettuce. As she ate it, listening to it crackle in her mouth, she looked around at the tables.

Hardly anyone was in there. She couldn't blame them for eating somewhere else. The menu was absolute trash. Sighing, Kate leaned back in her chair and pushed her plate away from her.

In the distance, she could see the sparkling pool. A couple of people were splashing around in there but most of the people were soaking up the sun on the loungers surrounding it.

All of it looked so peaceful, so dream-like. Kate wanted to go out there, to enjoy the sunshine on her skin, and figured that she may as well. She hadn't visited the pool yet and now looked like a good time to do it—since she'd arrived, she hadn't seen it this empty.

Kate had a couple more bites of her salad before getting up and heading out to the pool. The water reflected the sun's bright rays, stinging into her eyes. Kate made sure to look away from it as she walked around, heading for the first free lounger she could find.

There was one free, all on its own, toward the back of the area. It had plenty of sun, and its own little parasol to keep her cool if she needed it. Kate set her bag down on the floor beside her and immediately stretched out.

Her body warmed up quickly. It worked like a massage, getting rid of all the tension and knots in her body. Somewhere in the distance, she could hear ambient music playing. She glanced around, looking for a speaker, but gave up quickly. She didn't care where it was. All that mattered was the soft wooden sounds soothed her.

This is the life, Kate thought, sighing. *This is exactly what I needed.*

As she laid there, stretched out with her arms behind her head, she wondered how her daughter was getting along. She had exchanged the mandatory daily texts with her, but aside from that, she hadn't heard much.

It didn't matter, really. Claire was checking in regularly and that was all Kate asked for. Kate had to keep reminding herself that Claire was an adult now, perfectly capable of looking after herself, even if that meant spending all of her free time pining after a married man.

There was no point in her thinking about any of this. It was all out of her control. The only thing she could do was sit back, relax, and enjoy the remainder of her vacation. And that's exactly what Kate did.

A finger poked Kate roughly, right in the shoulder. She opened her eyes, not remembering when she'd closed them, and looked over at the person poking her.

It was just a young girl, only a couple of years older than Claire, frowning down at Kate.

"Miss," she was urging. "Miss, there are men asking for you."

*

Kate tried to clear her head and sat up in the recliner. "What?"

"Men," the girl repeated. "In the lobby. Asking for you."

"Men?" Kate asked. "For me?"

Nothing was making sense. The girl's beautiful black hair fell around the sides of her face, framing her tanned skin beautifully.

"Come," the girl said. "Two men. They won't leave the hotel."

Christ, Kate thought. *Who could that be, I wonder?*

There was no doubt in her mind that it was her previous night's conquest, coming back to haunt her. Why was it that men just couldn't let her go? They always had to come marching back, demanding more of her time and harassing those around her in the process.

Kate peeled herself off the lounger and put her purse over her shoulder, following the tiny girl back into the hotel. She didn't want to do this. She wanted to go back to the lounger, back to her dreamless sleep, but of course, life had a different plan for her.

As soon as she got into the lobby, and saw Fabian and Alessandro's bodies draped over the front desk, she could have snapped a neck. The rage appeared out of nowhere and burned through her body like a fire in the middle of a scorching summer.

When they saw her, they knew they'd fucked up. Their shit-eating grins were wiped off their faces. Kate waved them through the lobby curtly, before turning on her heels.

The only place she knew she could take them was the dining hall. It was long after lunch and they weren't still serving food. No one would be in there to overhear them.

They sat down opposite her with pale, sullen faces. Kate just stared at them, expecting them to explain why they were there.

"Hi," Fabian said softly.

"What do you want?" Kate snapped. "Why are you harassing the staff at my hotel?"

"We wanted to see you again," Alessandro said. "We tried calling your room number but nobody answered."

Kate's eyes darkened as she stared at them. "So what?" she asked. "I'm supposed to sit around in my hotel room waiting for your call?"

"No," Fabian started, "but—"

"Just tell me what you want," Kate blurted. "Please. Just tell me and let's get this over with."

"We want to see you again," Fabian said, sounding a little confused, his brows furrowed. "Do you not want to see us?"

"Sure," Kate said. "But not like this. The girl said you refused to leave without talking to me? Who *does* that?"

Neither of them had an answer for her. Kate could only roll her eyes.

"Well, clearly you two do that," she snapped.

"We've been talking about you all night," Alessandro said. "We just can't believe how fantastic you are. We want to spend more time with you. To get to know you better."

Kate felt her heart turn to stone inside of her. *Get to know me better? Oh, who do these boys think they're kidding?*

"Honey, no," Kate sighed. "We're not going to get to know each other any better than we already do."

Both of their faces fell, their dreams clearly crushed.

"I don't want to get to know either of you," Kate explained. "All I want is sex. Good sex. Sex like last night. Do you understand?"

The boys glanced at each other and silently conferred. To Kate, it looked like they were going to back out, but to her delight, they both nodded eagerly.

"Fine," Kate said. "If we are going to do this again, then we are going to do it my way."

"What does that mean?" Alessandro asked.

"It means there are going to be rules," Kate explained. "I've already had a lot of bad fucks this vacation and I'm not about to add two more to the list. Do you understand?"

The boys paused, looking uneasy. Fabian's thin eyebrows were so far up his head that Kate thought they might rocket off at any moment. Clearly, he'd never met a woman who knew exactly what she wanted and how she wanted it.

"I'm not playing," Kate said. "I'm not here to tolerate bad sex."

"What kind of rules?" Alessandro asked, hesitation lacing his voice.

"Both of you," Kate said. "At the same time. All three of us together. You will do what I say, when I say it, and you will do it immediately. Before we get naked, we will come up with hard and soft limits, a safe word, and I will tell you what kind of play I have in mind."

The boys had turned white as ghosts. Their faces were covered in sweat and Fabian's eyes were looking around them nervously, desperately trying to see if someone was nearby with a camera.

"Is this like... BDSM?" Alessandro asked. "'Cause I'm not into that."

"Me neither," Fabian added.

"No," Kate said. "I just want us all to have a good time and since you both have clearly never had a threesome, we need to do this right. I want you to both be submissive to me and do exactly as I say. How can I do that if I don't know what you're willing to do?"

Alessandro scoffed. "I'll do whatever you want," he said. "Anything for you."

"So, you'll suck Fabian's cock, then?" Kate asked, looking at Alessandro pointedly.

He instantly paled another shade, now looking almost gray and sickly. He gulped and leaned back into his chair, shaking his head gently.

"Didn't think so," Kate said, trying not to smirk. "This is why you need to come up with limits. Discuss them amongst each other. Make sure you're both on the same page."

Kate rose from the table and looked down to them, feeling her stomach tightening under the anticipation.

"Come to my hotel room tonight," she said. "Room seven-five-one."

There was nothing else to say to them. They had to do this part all on their own. Kate had no interest in listening to them bickering about what they were willing to do in each other's presence. So she left, making her way back to the hotel pool to relax before their big night.

Both of them would make an appearance, she knew that much. They were so desperate to see her, they'd make some kind of arrangement. Whatever that was, Kate could only wait and see.

For now, she let her body relax into a lounger as her skin soaked up the sun. It was deliriously hot, fueling the warmth spreading through her body, making its way down to between her legs.

There was no stopping that internal heat. All she wanted was some time with those boys, feeling their bodies pressed against hers as Fabian gave her more of the best head she'd ever had.

Stop, Kate thought.

If she continued thinking about it, she knew she'd end up soaking through her clothes. Fabian was just too good at it. Just remembering what he'd done to her body was too much to handle. Kate didn't understand how she'd even survived the night. Such intense orgasms that took hold of every inch of her.

She shook her head and moved both of her hands up, behind her head. She had to pin them down to stop them from making their way to her pussy. All she wanted was to touch herself but she couldn't do it in public, not unless she wanted her vacation cut short.

Kate couldn't take it, though. She could feel her pussy throbbing, pulsing, begging to be touched. Sitting in the sun wasn't going to get her what she needed.

Within a split second, she decided to leave. There were plenty more days for her to sit in the sun and do nothing. Today wasn't one of those days. She needed to get up to her hotel room and play with one of her toys. Waiting until tonight was out of the question—she needed relief and she needed it *now*.

Kate made it up to her hotel room quickly, feeling her legs rub together as she rushed all the way up to the right floor. As soon as she was inside the room, the air conditioner blew cold air into her face and sent shivers all down her skin.

She stood there for a moment, enjoying the feeling, before climbing onto the bed. Instantly her hands dived beneath her pants, searching for her pussy. When her fingers were close, she could feel her arousal. Her underwear was soaked and her skin was warm and throbbing.

There was no time for toys or lube or porn. She pressed her fingers into her clitoris and began to rub. She started off slow, but even that wasn't enough. She needed more pressure, more tension, more everything.

Kate's stomach was tied in knots and her legs were shaking as she continued to move her fingers diagonally across herself. All of the muscles in her body were climbing to that glorious point, tensing up for the inevitable release.

It came over her so suddenly. Kate let out a choked moan as she felt her whole body spasm. She slowed her hand as she rode the wave, feeling every inch of her body tingling.

Chapter Seventeen

Toyboys

THEY WERE QUIVERING IN front of her, down on their knees, naked as the day they were born. Kate couldn't help but smile as she looked at them—at their faces, at the way their bottom lips trembled.

Kate didn't know whether it was anticipation or dread. She didn't care either way. They'd agreed to this and now they were going to get what they had so desperately wanted.

They'd already talked about their limits, agreed upon a safe word, and done all of the boring preparations. Now it was time for Kate to have her fun. And, hopefully, for the boys to have their fun as well.

As far as she could tell, they didn't look prepared to have fun. They almost looked frightened, like lost little boys pining for their mothers. It didn't matter. Soon enough they'd be having more than enough fun.

Kate felt her bare legs brush together as she began to walk around them, her high-heeled shoes digging into the carpet below her. Her hand brushed along the boy's shoulders as she passed behind them, sending goosebumps all down their backs.

Fabian was keeping his eyes turned down, already meek and submissive for her. Alessandro was more cocky and confident, looking up to her and letting his eyes follow her around the room.

He needed to be broken in. He needed to be put in his place and shown how he should act in her presence. She wanted to shove her pussy in his face and ride him until he was defeated, but she could still feel Fabian's tongue on her body.

Everything about him was so appetizing. He drew her in so easily, with his oral skills and his basic body, and his submissive attitude. Almost everything about him was so perfect.

Kate could feel herself getting attached to him. That was something that she never allowed herself to feel. She didn't need a man in her life—she was here to use them and toss them aside—so letting this one get close to her was out of the question.

She let her hands run through Alessandro's hair, tugging at it gently as she moved in front of him. He looked up to her, his mouth set in a hard line.

"Lick me," Kate breathed.

Alessandro didn't need to be told twice. He lurched forward and wrapped his lips around her clit. He let his tongue explore her, its warmth spreading all over her as he began to circle her. Kate could feel the pleasure, feel it rising up her body as he started to suck, but he was nowhere near as good as Fabian.

When Alessandro wound his hands around Kate's waist, pulling her body tighter against his face, she looked down at him, frowning.

Without warning, she slapped both of his hands and pried them off her body.

He was stunned—he looked up to her with wide eyes, his mouth hanging open.

"I didn't say you could touch," Kate said. "Continue."

Alessandro put his hands on his lap and struggled to clamp his mouth around Kate's pussy. As he worked on her, all she could think about was Fabian's wonderful mouth.

She glanced over at him. He was staring at Alessandro, watching what he was doing. There was no judgment in his eyes, not that Kate could see, but she knew that he could do this better.

Kate wasn't going to stand for mediocrity. She clutched Alessandro's hair between her fingers and threw his head back, almost knocking him off his knees. He stumbled back and watched in horror as Kate stood in front of Fabian.

"Are you serious?" Alessandro said, his voice loud and raised. "You barely gave me a cha—"

Kate slapped him across the cheek. Not too hard, but hard enough that their skin connecting made a loud clapping sound. Alessandro looked up to her, dazed, as he held his reddening cheek.

"Shush," Kate said. "Sit. Wait."

As soon as she positioned herself in front of Fabian, he got to work. His tongue knew exactly what to do and where to go. No questions, no urging, just straight to the point.

Kate felt her body start to melt as he flicked his tongue across her clitoris, tasting her juices as she grew more aroused. She could feel herself start to drip down her inner thighs as Fabian worked on her, keeping his hands clasped in his lap.

The heat came quickly, followed almost instantly by the sweat. Her muscles tensed as the orgasm came close, edging toward her with every move of Fabian's tongue.

Before he could make her cum, she moved away. It was hard, but she wasn't going to let herself finish that quickly. After all, they'd only just begun.

Fabian didn't look hurt, confused, or much of anything. He stayed on his knees and watched her with eagle eyes. Alessandro, kneeling next to him, was keeping his eyes down to the floor. It seemed like all of his enthusiasm was gone.

"Are you upset over a little slap?" Kate asked, talking to him in a gentle, soothing tone. "Little Alessandro's ego bruised?"

He gritted his teeth together and said nothing. Kate could see him holding himself back, tensing and releasing all of the muscles in his arms. She let her teeth sink into her bottom lip as she looked down at him, her hand touching the cheek she'd just slapped.

"Your turn again," she said.

Alessandro moved to her aggressively, shoving his head between her legs and craning his neck back so far Kate thought it might snap. She wasn't worried about that for long. His tongue explored her, lapping at her clitoris slowly, teasing her a little.

Whatever he was doing, he was getting better. Kate let her head lean back a little as she enjoyed the feeling of his tongue licking at her body. She could feel him wanting to wrap his hands around her body but he didn't. He did as he was told, keeping his hands firmly in his lap.

Eventually, he managed to get Kate to break out into a sweat. She was gasping with her mouth open and her eyes closed, letting her own fingers play with her nipples.

Again, she could feel the orgasm coming. She wasn't about to let that happen, though. She stepped away from Alessandro, watching as he almost fell face-first into the carpet, and stood in front of Fabian again.

She knew that this time she was probably going to cum. Both boys had brought her close and this time was going to be the icing on the cake. She looked down into Fabian's steady eyes.

"You know what to do," she said gently.

Fabian licked her, more enthusiastically than before. His tongue went to all the right places, circling around her clitoris before darting away, down between her lips to taste her juices.

He brought Kate onto the brink of orgasm. Her whole body was shaking, struggling to stand upright, as her legs quivered. She could barely focus on anything aside from the feeling between her legs. All she could think about was Fabian's magic tongue, delving deep inside of her.

She had to yank herself away before she came. That wasn't how she wanted tonight to go. She was gasping for air as she flapped her hand in front of her face, trying to cool herself down.

When she regained her composure, she saw that Fabian had his cock in his hand, grabbing it tightly and yanking on it.

“Did I say you could touch yourself?” Kate snapped.

Fabian instantly let go of himself. Kate could see a small bead of pre-cum on the tip, glistening in the light. She shook her head slowly as she stared at it disapprovingly.

When she turned her eyes to Alessandro, she looked down between his legs and saw that he barely had an erection. She raised her right eyebrow as she looked at it.

“Am I not turning you on?” she asked.

Kate knelt down in front of him and looked into his eyes. She pushed his body back so he was sitting on his ankles. Then she put her knees on either side of his thighs. With both of her hands on his shoulders, she lowered her pussy against his limp cock, covering it in her arousal.

Ever so slowly, she moved her hips forward and back, thrusting into his stomach as her pussy ground against his cock. Within a couple of seconds, she could feel it growing beneath her, pulsing full of blood and promise.

Kate smiled at him. “That’s better,” she purred. “So much better.”

Alessandro’s hands hovered over her hips, desperate to grab hold of her and help her grind her pussy against his cock, but he stopped himself. Kate smiled widely as she continued to ride him, feeling his cock grow and throb beneath her.

Only when he was fully erect did she climb off him. There was no need to keep teasing him when all his blood was in the right place. She stood between them and looked at them in turn, wondering what she could get them to do next.

Kate didn't know what she was in the mood for. The only thing she could think about was Fabian's perfect mouth, the shapes it made, the way it made her feel. But that wasn't fair to Alessandro. He was the more eager of the two and he deserved to be praised for that.

Kate climbed back onto the bed with her elbows propping up her body. She spread her legs slowly. Both boys looked straight at her pussy. Fabian had the audacity to lick his lips. Kate felt a tingle down there as her body yearned for his touch.

"Alessandro," she said, "there's a little box in the dresser behind you. Get it."

He didn't waste any time. He jumped to his feet, his cock bouncing in the air as he moved, and brought out Kate's box of toys. He set it on the bed between her legs and stepped away as if he was scared to be too close to her.

"Open it," she said. "Take out a toy. Your choice."

Alessandro looked like a deer in headlights for a moment. He didn't know where to put his hands, or what to touch, but he eventually settled on a little egg-shaped vibrator.

Kate grinned at him. "Do you have any idea what that is?"

"No," he gulped.

“Come here,” Kate purred. “I’ll show you.”

Alessandro knelt on the edge of the bed beside her, his eyes drifting up and down her naked body. Kate felt a thrill go through her. It was clear he liked what he saw.

Kate turned the vibrating egg on, licked her fingers, and smeared her saliva all over clit. Then she pressed the egg against the side of her clitoris.

She had trouble keeping it in place. It felt too good. Almost as good as Fabian’s mouth. She felt her legs tighten as it brought her close to orgasm. Alessandro’s hands took over, holding the egg against her skin, as her whole body started to shiver.

Then he moved it to the other side of her, causing Kate’s stomach to clench wildly. She felt her whole body rising like a wave, just waiting for everything to crash down as the orgasm built up.

Suddenly the vibrations vanished, leaving her body reeling. She looked up and saw Alessandro’s grinning face. His hands were holding the egg in the air. After a second, Kate realized that he was teasing her.

Kate sat up in the bed and snatched the egg out of Alessandro’s hand. Then she planted her bare foot in the center of his chest and gently pushed, signaling for him to get off the bed.

“Fabian,” Kate whispered his name. “Join me.”

Alessandro’s face was filled with despair. He sat at the end of the bed on the floor like a sulking child. Fabian climbed onto the bed and positioned his mouth between her legs, ready to fuck her with his mouth.

Kate didn't need to say anything—he already knew what she wanted. She wrapped her legs around the sides of his head and let her feet dangle down his back.

Fabian's tongue explored her, but now it knew her intimately. It knew exactly where to go and what to do to get her off. Within a couple of seconds, he had Kate panting and sweating. Her body was writhing as she felt the orgasm rising up once more.

Fabian made her cum harder than he had before. Her whole body twitched and spasmed as the orgasm took control of her whole body. All of the muscles in her pelvis went numb as they tensed and released repetitively. A long, soft groan came out of her mouth as she lost complete control of her body.

She was too sensitive to continue, so she pushed Fabian's mouth away as she rolled around on the bed, groaning as her muscles were still out of control. Her whole body shivered and shook as she looked up to the ceiling, wondering how she'd gotten so lucky to find a mouth like his.

Fabian moved his body up hers, ready to start again, but Kate just pushed him away again. She needed a moment to recuperate. The orgasm was still causing havoc in her body, making her muscles twinge and tense.

All she could do was relax on the bed with her limbs spread out as she tried to calm her beating heart and ragged breaths. She kept her eyes focused on the white, plain ceiling as she tried to calm down. Looking at it made her feel bored and that was one quick way to get her body to return to normal.

"What did you do?" Alessandro asked, whispering. "How the hell did you break her like that?"

Kate didn't hear Fabian reply. She assumed he either was keeping his mouth shut, as he was told, or he just shrugged.

What she didn't understand was how such a shy, timid boy could have a skill like that so naturally. What was even worse was he'd probably never used that skill to its greatest potential.

How many women missed out on the most mind-blowing orgasms of their lives, simply because they wouldn't go for someone like Fabian?

Kate finally got control of her body back. She wiped the sweat from her forehead and sat up in the bed, hardly able to catch her breath. Both of the boys looked to her, waiting for instruction.

Chapter Eighteen

A hole is a hole

KATE PERCHED ON THE end of the bed as she rummaged through her box of toys. She was looking for the small package of condoms that she'd brought. She knew she had them in there, somewhere. It was a selection box, a mix-and-match of sorts. Ribbed, ultra-thin, flavored. Everything a girl could need.

When she finally found the packet and looked up, Alessandro was standing to the side of her, watching her with glistening eyes. He looked uncomfortable, with the corners of his mouth pulled down and his brows furrowed deeply.

"Is this how you get off?" he asked. "Abusing men?"

Kate tilted her head to the side as she stood up, staring at him. "Is this abuse to you?" she asked. "I told you to go over your hard limits and I haven't crossed them. Have I?"

"No, but—"

"So, you're *feeling* abused?" Kate asked, urging him to answer.

“I mean—”

"So, you don’t feel abused,” Kate started, “you like what’s happening here, but you’re not comfortable with it. Is that it?”

Alessandro didn’t want to nod, but Kate could see it in his eyes—she’d gotten it right.

“That’s your ego,” Kate whispered, taking a step closer to him. “The terrible male ego, telling you that *you* should be the one with all the power, not me.”

“How does that make a differ—”

“Because,” Kate interrupted, “I’m not abusing you. I’m *dominating* you.”

Kate put her hand on Alessandro’s chest and pushed gently. She watched as he sank to his knees in front of her, his cock turning limp with every second that passed. Kate paid no attention to it as she walked circles around him, letting her hands brush over his soft shoulders.

“All my life, men have been dominating me,” Kate said slowly. “In every aspect of every inch of my life, men have told me what to do, what to wear, how to act, how to live.

“I don’t want my life to be run by men, but I have no choice. My superiors at work are all men, my colleagues are all men, and the people I manage are mostly men.”

Kate looked down at Alessandro, peering into his eyes. She couldn’t tell what he was thinking or feeling, but that didn’t really matter.

"I don't want to be ruled by men, so I enjoy my free time like this," she said. I like to have my way with men. I like what I like and I like men to do what I ask. Is that really so bad?"

It sounded like a question, but she wasn't about to give him the chance to reply. Kate knelt down in front of him and grabbed his face with her fingers, squishing his lips together until they popped out of his mouth like a duck's beak.

"Besides, you were so eager to be here," Kate continued. "You convinced Fabian to go through with this. Now he's more excited about this than you are."

Kate let go of his face, almost shoving him backward, and stood up. As she looked down at him, she knew what he needed. It wasn't convincing that he needed—it was reminding.

"Get up," Kate snapped.

Alessandro reluctantly got to his feet. Kate put her hands on his waist and dragged him toward her. His limp cock swayed between his legs as he walked. Kate looked at it and brought up a swarm of saliva into her mouth.

Before she let it inside of her, she had to get it hard first. There was nothing in this world that she hated more than a soft cock in her mouth. So, she grabbed hold of him and began to pump.

She wasn't gentle with him. She used a hard grip and moved her arm ferociously, glancing up at Alessandro occasionally. His mouth opened wide and stayed open as short little gasps escaped him.

His cock grew quickly in her hand, more than doubling in size. When Kate was satisfied, she leaned forward and stuck his cock in her mouth.

She could taste his salty skin against her tongue and she could feel his body reacting to her mouth, his cock pulsing as she let her tongue roam around it.

When she tasted the incredibly salty pre-cum in her mouth, Kate knew she needed to stop. She moved her head away from Alessandro's cock and let it fall out of her mouth. Then she stood up and forced him to sit on the bed.

"You're mine," she whispered, pushing her hands into his shoulders and forcing him to lie down on the bed.

Once he was reclined with his eyes closed, Kate got to her knees and began to suck him off again. This time, she waved Fabian over. He sat beside her, waiting for instruction.

Kate took Alessandro's cock down into the back of her throat, causing her to gag a little. She controlled the sound and kept his cock down. When she moved her head away, she looked over to Fabian and nodded for him to continue where she'd left off.

To her surprise, he didn't balk or turn pale at her suggestion. They switched places without Alessandro knowing and Fabian took his friend's cock in his mouth.

Just watching those sweet lips wrap around Alessandro's thick cock was incredibly exciting to Kate. She could see Fabian's mouth opening wide as Alessandro's cock went deep down into his throat.

Kate felt her pussy start to pulse as she watched them. She had no idea how exciting it was to watch two men together, or how much it turned her on.

She sat back in one of the chairs next to the bed and watched them for a while. Alessandro was enjoying himself more now than before when Kate had been the one sucking him off.

She didn't take offense to it—men knew what men liked. After all, they had the same equipment. It was only fair that Alessandro got to know just how magical Fabian's mouth was.

After a while, she saw Fabian stroking his own cock, trying to keep himself hard. Kate lifted herself off the chair and sat beside Fabian. She removed his hand from his member and replaced it with hers while he continued to work.

After a minute, Kate knew that she wanted to taste Fabian's cock again. It wasn't as monstrous as Alessandro's but it was just as nice. She leaned her body down, slipping between the bed and Fabian's knees, and took his cock into her mouth.

Despite the awkward positioning, she managed to do the job well enough to make Fabian moan. The vibrations rolled through his mouth and around Alessandro's cock, which made him groan in turn.

Kate knew that he was going to look up soon, that he was going to see his friend's head with his lips wrapped around his dick, but she didn't care. He'd been enjoying it, so why would seeing a man down there make a difference? A hole was a hole, after all.

When Kate's jaw became tense and sore from all the sucking, she knew she needed to stop this madness and finally feel their cocks inside of her pussy. She needed them to fill her up in every sense of the word.

She slipped away from Fabian and watched them for a moment more, enjoying the beautiful sight.

"All right," Kate said. "That's enough, boys."

Confused, Alessandro leaned his head up and looked at where Kate's voice had come from. His brows tightened together as he stared at her, clearly bewildered. Then he felt the mouth wrapped around his dick and looked down.

When his eyes settled on Fabian's face, they widened in shock. His mouth opened as he gasped in horror and his body tried to wriggle away. Kate wasn't going to stand for that.

She moved over to them and pushed on the back of Fabian's head, forcing Alessandro's cock into the depths of his throat.

"Don't you move," she purred. "You've been enjoying it all this time."

From below, she could hear Fabian spluttering as Alessandro's cock stayed so far down in his throat. She paid the sounds no mind as she continued to stare at Alessandro's face.

"There's nothing wrong with boys loving boys," Kate said with a smile. "You know that, don't you?"

She let go of Fabian's head and, to her surprise, he continued blowing his friend. Alessandro's eyes rolled into the back of his head at the feeling, his body shuddering as he prepared to cum.

Kate didn't move to stop it. She watched as it took hold of Alessandro, his seed spurting down Fabian's mouth and throat. It was all done in a couple of seconds and Fabian moved away before swallowing the load.

Breathlessly, Alessandro laid back on the bed and let his hands touch his forehead, rubbing his hair back from his skin. Sweat covered his muscled body, making it shine under the bright, white lights in the room.

Kate couldn't help but feel satisfied with herself. Not only had she managed to get two straight men to fuck each other, but she'd also probably ruined this friendship. It was a nasty thing to think but she couldn't help getting a kick out of it. Who wouldn't enjoy having so much power?

"Now your turn," she said to Fabian.

His eyes bulged and glanced back to Alessandro. Instead of shock, or disgust, she saw acceptance in his eyes. Alessandro instantly got down onto the floor and waited for Fabian to sit on the edge of the bed.

As soon as they were in position, with Fabian's erect cock standing tall in the air, Alessandro's mouth wrapped around it and began to suck as if his life depended on it.

Kate felt her whole body respond to the sight. Her pussy clenched and started to drip again, and a nervous energy burst into her stomach. These boys were hers, wholly and completely, and once Fabian had his first orgasm of the night, they would be able to move on.

For whatever reason, Fabian had a harder time letting himself go. He couldn't get lost in the moment. He was so focused on his friend between his legs that he couldn't sustain his erection.

Kate intervened only then. She sat on his stomach and pushed her pussy against his skin. He looked up at her, his hands grabbing her thighs and breasts.

The fires started to burn inside him again. Kate leaned down to kiss him and let her tongue dance with his. Behind her, she could hear Alessandro's mouth taking in Fabian's cock, harder and deeper.

It was working. Her presence was helping him along. All she had to do was keep him entertained and distracted and soon he would shoot his load into his friend's mouth.

She allowed Fabian's fingers to work her clitoris, and his hands to explore her body. She didn't care and relinquished a little control. If she wanted the rest of the night to continue as she wanted to, it was necessary.

Fabian's mouth opened up as she was kissing him and puffs of air shot into her mouth. Kate leaned back to look at him and saw he had squeezed his eyes shut.

"I'm gonna—" was all he managed to say before a long, aching groan replaced his words.

Kate looked over her shoulder and saw a similar expression on Alessandro's face. Without a doubt, Fabian had just ejaculated. She continued to watch as Alessandro struggled to swallow it. It took him a couple of tries before he managed, swallowing the load down with a grimace.

"Fuck," Fabian whispered. "Fuck, fuck, fuck."

Kate detached herself from his body and looked at the both of them, a smug smile on her lips. She'd broken them and bent them to her will. There was no other way of describing it. These boys had done the unthinkable for her, for just one night of pleasure.

Both of them were covered in sweat, their bodies shaking and their eyes wide and glassy. Kate could see that nothing would ever be the same for them, ever again. She'd ruined their innocent minds and now she would show them a world of pleasure that they had never thought existed.

Kate laid down on the bed and stretched out as she stared at the boys. They both looked tired, exhausted almost, and their spirits were clearly drained.

"Come," she said, holding her arms out for both of them. "Come and lie with me a while."

They didn't argue. They didn't put up a fight. Both of them slithered up the bed and lodged themselves beneath her armpits, snuggling their heads on each side of her shoulder.

Kate wrapped her arms around their backs as all three of them closed their eyes and relaxed. She could feel their wet, slick, limp cocks pressing against her thighs.

She knew that soon enough they would start to get hard again, and this time they wouldn't cum so fast. There was only a small window for her to relax and enjoy the feeling of their warm bodies pressed against hers.

It only took ten minutes for Fabian's fingers to begin exploring her body, slipping down between her legs so quickly. Kate wasn't going to argue with him. They had done so much for her already and they were still willing to do more. Only a cruel mistress would punish them for that.

When Alessandro realized what Fabian was doing, he joined in on the fun. He put his hand on Kate's breast, his fingers playing with her nipple, tugging on it and twisting it.

All of a sudden, all the attention was back on Kate. Her chest started to heave as her body was worked on. Fabian's fingers felt her slickness and plunged deep inside of her with his thumb pressed against her clit.

Alessandro moved down to let his mouth wrap around her nipple, licking and sucking at it until he was as hard as a rock against her thigh.

Kate couldn't believe how quickly they were able to stand to attention and she wanted to take their cocks into her mouth, into her body. There was no way she was going to be able to wait any longer. She had to have them, and now.

Before she had a chance to get up off the bed and demand a fucking, Fabian slipped down and put his lips around her pussy. Kate's mouth popped open at the feeling and all of her body turned hot to the touch.

Fabian's tongue lapped at her, twisting around her before his mouth sucked on her and his teeth nibbled at her. It was almost too much for her to take.

Within minutes, Fabian had her cumming so hard she thought she was going to pass out. She gripped onto the bed sheets below as her whole body tensed and released, causing her to quiver and shake.

Chapter Nineteen

Goddess energy

Kate let herself recover for a while before moving on with the evening. She was already feeling tired and incredibly achy, but she couldn't let the boys down. The evening had only just begun. She just needed a couple of minutes to catch her breath and wipe the sweat off her body.

Fabian and Alessandro were perched on either side of her, staring at her face and body as their hands roamed over her skin. They were clearly waiting for her to tell them what to do, but she just wasn't ready yet. Her heart was still pounding. If she had any more excitement, it felt like her heart would explode.

It was clear to her that she'd broken through their egos and demolished the walls they'd built around themselves. All they wanted was to please her, to be with her, to do everything she wanted of them.

Kate couldn't believe how successful this had been. As she gazed between their faces, she remembered how stiff they had both been that first night they met. Even giving them a blowjob out in the open was too much for them to handle. Now they'd sucked each other off, just for her.

Now that her heart had calmed down a little, she shifted her body on the bed. Both of the boys instantly got up onto their knees, ready to please her. They were so eager, so ready for her, it didn't feel quite right.

Kate felt a little uneasy with how willing they were, but she tried to push the thoughts aside as she got onto her knees. Without having to ask, both boys positioned themselves in front of her and started pumping their cocks with their hands.

Another uneasy feeling washed over her, but this time it was stronger. Their naked bodies were so close, their hands brushing against each other as they jerked themselves off. Kate knew that only a few hours ago they would never have dreamed of doing anything like that.

She couldn't understand what she was feeling. Everything that she'd wanted had happened: they had changed completely for her, willing to do whatever she wanted... so why wasn't she happy?

The cocks were growing in front of her. She couldn't ignore them anymore. Kate had nothing else to do but open her mouth and let the boys shove their cocks inside.

Once again she could taste their skin—salty but sweet—but her heart just wasn't in it. She felt almost depressed, sucking because the cocks were there and not because she wanted to.

Still, Kate persisted. She sucked as best as she could, shoving their cocks inside her mouth in turn, taking them deep down her throat. Both the boys groaned and moaned as she worked on them but the sounds coming out of their mouths didn't turn her on as much as they had.

It was as if the boys had outlived their usefulness to her and now they were boring. Kate tried not to let the thoughts get to her but they just kept coming, swarming over her and taking control of her mind and body.

There was only one way she was going to get these thoughts to disappear for once and for all—she was going to have to fuck them, to have their cocks inside of her holes.

Kate removed her mouth from Fabian's cock and got onto her knees. For a moment, she considered kicking them out of the hotel room altogether. She imagined their shocked, hurt faces as she shoved them out of the room.

A smile crept onto her lips as she thought about it. The boys touched her breasts and stomach, waiting for her to come back to them. Kate looked between them for a moment, before leaning down on her elbows, her ass in the air.

"Fuck me," she stated, her voice almost bland and monotone.

The boys rushed off the bed and collected their condoms. It only took them a couple of seconds to get them on, sliding the latex over their shafts. When they were covered completely, they edged toward her sheepishly.

"Fuck me," Kate stated again, this time with more aggression and passion.

She was done waiting. She wanted the boys to fuck her and finish the entire evening off. They climbed onto the bed, with Fabian behind her and Alessandro in front.

As she opened her mouth to Alessandro's cock, she felt Fabian enter her from behind. She squeezed her eyes shut as his cock gently eased inside of her, opening her up as it continued to push through.

Kate wasn't about to give up all of her control, though. Instead of letting them thrust into her, Kate moved her body between them. Leaning forward, she took Alessandro's cock deep into her throat. Then, when she leaned back, she felt Fabian's cock delve into her.

She started off slow, keeping her pace, making sure that both of them were ready to finally fuck her. Fabian placed his hands on her hips, cementing his body to hers, but Alessandro kept his hands at the base of his shaft.

Kate propelled her body back and forth, feeling a cock sliding into her at either end as she moved. The feeling was a little strange but not unpleasant.

She could feel Alessandro's large cock sliding farther down her throat with every thrust, threatening to choke her. Fabian's hip bones pressed into her ass every time she slammed her body backward.

Kate made sure to keep control over them as she fucked them both, moving her body between theirs in a smooth, rocking motion. She got faster and faster, moving her body so quickly that she began to sweat from exertion.

Fabian was the first to blow his load. His fingers dug into her hips as he started to cum. Kate felt it and began to slam her ass against his pelvis, making sure to give him a great orgasm.

He groaned loudly as his cock pulsed inside of her. Kate felt relieved that he had finished but she was a little disappointed he hadn't lasted into the final show.

He withdrew from her, sighing and gasping, before lying down on the bed next to her, watching her suck Alessandro's cock. She wasn't going to do this for much longer, though.

She moved her mouth away from his member and looked up at him.

"Get behind me," she said.

Alessandro didn't need any more prompting. He switched to behind her and pushed his latex-clad cock against her pussy.

"Wrong hole," Kate said curtly, looking over her shoulder at him.

She saw him back there, behind her ass, bemused. She nodded slowly, urging him on, and felt his cock slip up a little, aiming right for her backdoor.

He paused there a moment, holding himself against the hole. "Are you sure?"

Kate spun her head around and shot daggers out of her eyes. "I know what I'm doing," she snapped. "A hole is a hole. Now fuck it!"

Alessandro wasn't about to argue again. He began to push inside, taking it very slowly. All Kate could do was let her head relax against the bed as she felt Alessandro enter a place very few men had gone.

She always saved anal for a special occasion and tonight was special. If Fabian had lasted just a bit longer, he'd been able to enjoy this as well.

Shame, she thought, sighing. *He won't get another chance like this.*

When Alessandro's cock was fully inside, his hips pressed against her cheeks, she felt him start to spasm. Kate looked over her shoulder at him and opened her mouth to speak, but it was already too late.

Alessandro began to shout out as he came explosively inside of her, his cock pulsing as his whole body twitched and shook. He kept his eyes shut as he grabbed her hips, riding out the orgasm.

Fabian sat up on the bed and looked at Kate's ass, his eyes wide. "Is anal really that good?"

Kate shrugged. "Maybe," she said. "You missed out, it seems."

Alessandro hissed as he pulled his cock out of her. It was already turning limp. He tossed the condom into the trash and climbed onto the bed, his eyes glistening and full of adoration.

Kate climbed up the bed herself and laid in the middle of it, needing a little time to relax. The boys positioned themselves on either side of her, their arms wrapped around her naked body as they snuggled up close.

It didn't feel right to Kate, though. The closer they came to her, the more she wanted to kick them off. Having two men in bed with her, cuddling her, brushing the hair away from her eyes... It all felt so foreign, so wrong.

All her life she'd never needed a man to complete her and that was never going to change. She came on vacation to enjoy herself and that's exactly what she had done.

So, why did she feel the need to keep these boys around her for a little longer? Was it for them? It was clear they held some affection for her but she felt nothing of the like.

In fact, the men here had been such a good distraction for her that she hadn't thought about work all that much at all. They'd done their job—they'd cleared her head and given her multiple orgasms. Why was she keeping them around?

Kate sat up in the bed, unable to shake the thoughts from her mind. She peeled the boy's hands off her body and stood up from the bed, heading into the bathroom.

She splashed some water on her face and rubbed her hands all over her skin, trying to wake herself up from this weird, fuzzy mental state she found herself in.

Dark blue eyes stared out of the mirror, surrounded by her deeply tanned skin covered in freckles and beauty marks. Wavy brown hair puffed out of her head at either side in a knotted, scraggly mess. Her cheeks were flushed from all the excitement and her eyes were dilated and dark.

As she stared at herself, she tried to figure out why she wanted to keep the boys here when they had served their purpose. Did she feel guilty? Or lonely? Did she miss her daughter, her only family, and want to replace her presence with fucktoys?

Kate didn't know, and she didn't really want to find out. She dried off her face and left the bathroom with a robe wrapped around her body. As soon as she was out of the bathroom, the boys lunged to the edge of the bed, their big eyes begging her for more.

Kate felt repulsed by the way they looked at her. Begging beasts, asking *please may we have some more?* It was pathetic. And Kate couldn't believe she'd turned Alessandro into such a creature.

She looked at them, trying not to grimace. "You boys have to leave now," she said slowly.

Their faces fell in unison. Fabian kicked his legs over the edge of the bed, suddenly looking defeated.

"This has been lovely," she said slowly, "but I'm tired now and I need some rest."

"We can stay here," Alessandro said quickly, "with you... I mean, if you want."

"If I wanted company I would have asked for it," Kate said. "Please leave now."

Fabian didn't argue. He just started collecting his clothes in silence. Alessandro had a spirited look in his eyes, like he was about to start shouting or making a scene. He stepped up to Kate, trying to intimidate her with his height and width, but she just stared at him in reply.

As if a little boy like him could scare her. She ate bigger men for breakfast back at work, and that was the truth. The men she faced every day were much more domineering and intimidating than these two.

If she could wrap these two around her fingers with ease, why couldn't she do it with those idiots at work? All she needed to do was channel her inner goddess, channel her dominatrix, channel every piece of herself into her work. They wouldn't know what hit them.

Fabian was dressed, ready to leave, but Alessandro was still throwing a silent fit. He was staring at Kate angrily as he stepped into his pants. She didn't care. There was nothing she could do to make him feel better and there was nothing she *wanted* to do.

When the hotel door slammed shut behind her, she let out a sigh of relief. She had the room to herself, finally. Now she could relax, read some emails, and get back into the right state of mind.

Finally, she could prepare to go home.

Chapter Twenty

Let's begin

All Kate wanted to do was get back home and relax but life kept getting in the way. The flight was delayed while they were waiting on the runway, making Kate's legs jitter as she sat in her seat trying to wait patiently.

Once they finally got up into the air, the flight had been painfully long. She hadn't remembered it being so long on the way over, but on the way back it was almost intolerable. She just couldn't handle it—she was done with this vacation already, she just wanted it all to be behind her.

As she sat in her seat, twisting her fingers around each other as her legs shook beneath her, she thought about everything she'd done wrong on the vacation. Not only had she made the stupid mistake of sleeping with idiots, but she'd somehow managed to make two men fall head-over-heels in love with her.

That wasn't something that she needed, and it wasn't something she was looking for. All she wanted to do was just go back to her daughter and live her normal life.

Kate frowned. *Do I, though?*

The longer she thought about it, the more she realized that she didn't want to go back to her normal life. In fact, she wanted things to drastically change. Not only did she want to show the men at work that she was capable and didn't want to take their crap anymore, but she also wanted to show the same to her daughter.

Claire had been living her own life since she was fifteen years old. It wasn't right for Kate to take such a backseat in parenting her, but she'd always written it off.

She'd tell herself that Claire was a good kid, that she got good grades, and she would never come home pregnant. As if that was enough to warrant her hands-off parenting style.

Kate knew it was wrong to take that kind of approach, even if it had given her an easy life for the past three years. That needed to end—now. As soon as she got home, she was going to tell Claire exactly what needed to be said.

The journey home from the airport was long and arduous. Despite the fact that it was early in the morning, the traffic was horrific. It felt like Kate was stuck in the car at a standstill for the entire journey, edging along the road a couple of feet at a time.

By the time she got into the house, her bags dropped on the floor just behind the door, Kate let out a heavy sigh and stood in the middle of the entrance hall, her eyes closed as she breathed steadily.

When she was ready to open her eyes and look around, she saw that the house was just as she'd left it. Everything was in its right place. There was no mess, no trash, nothing broken. It was clear Claire hadn't had any parties here, or if she had, she'd cleaned up well.

By the lack of sounds coming from the house, it was clear that Claire wasn't home. Kate picked up her bags and brought them upstairs, ready to start unpacking and doing laundry. It wasn't the most fun chore in the world, but it needed to get done.

Once everything had been removed from her bags and put into the laundry basket, Kate pulled her laptop out of its carrier case and plugged it into the wall. She perched on the edge of her bed and waited for it to boot up.

It had been a while since she'd even bothered to look at it. She wondered how many emails had gone unread, unanswered, and ignored. Kate was a little worried about it. For all she knew, she'd been fired while she was on vacation.

Hundreds of emails were waiting for her. Kate groaned as she scrolled through the long list. She caught a couple of the titles. Most of them were innocuous enough, just updates and reports on how her team was doing.

A couple of emails stood out to her—conversations from her colleagues that she'd been added into that made it seem like they weren't missing her at all. Nasty comments about her vacation, her work ethic, how she'd thrown them under the bus by leaving so suddenly.

Kate could only grit her teeth as she skimmed through them, shaking her head slowly. They knew they had included her in the conversation, so why did they think it was okay to talk about her like this? Was she really that much of a pushover at work? Did they really behave like this all the time?

As she tried to remember what it was like working at her company before she'd gone on vacation, she heard the front door slam shut. Her eyes ripped from the laptop and focused on her bedroom door. For a moment, she listened intently as her daughter came into the house, kicking off her shoes and sighing as she moved through to the kitchen.

This was it. Kate's time to shine. She needed to step up and be a parent now, even if it fell on deaf ears. Claire couldn't continue seeing her married man. It was wrong and she needed to hear it.

Kate darted out of her bedroom and barreled down the stairs, just in time to see Claire walk into the living room. It took a second for her to register her mother's footsteps. She looked up at her, like a deer in headlights.

"Mom," she said slowly. "You're home?"

"Yes," Kate replied, stepping down the stairs as fast as she could, her eyes locked with Claire's. "And we need to talk."

"Now?" Claire asked, lifting her upper lip as she grimaced. "Can it not wait till, like, later?"

It was then that Kate realized there was someone else in the room with them.

Kate's eyes drifted over to the center of the living room, where she saw Claire's lover rising from the couch. His black hair was speckled with gray and his forehead was covered in deep grooves in his skin.

Kate pressed her lips together as she stared at the man. He had a strong jaw paired with oddly thin lips. Pale skin and freckles covered his face and his light blue eyes darted between them.

What could she say? It was blatantly obvious why they were both here, to enjoy the house while Kate was gone. But being faced with the older man who was preying on her young daughter stirred something inside Kate.

It had been just barely okay when it was an abstract thought, something she could think about without actually having to see, but now it was standing in her living room, a fire burned through her veins. And not the good kind.

"Is this him?" Kate asked, staring him up and down.

The top three buttons of his shirt were undone, revealing the dark hair on his chest, curly and wild. He was wearing an expensive suit, clearly having come straight from his work.

Claire only stared at her mother, her mouth hanging open.

"Is this *him*?" Kate asked, staring to Claire. "Answer me."

"How do you know about this?" Claire asked. "I've never told you anything."

Kate scoffed. "Do you think you're that sneaky?" Kate couldn't hold back the laughter. "You're eighteen, Claire. You're not so slick."

"I've never..." Claire searched for the words, searched for the comeback. "I never said a word to you. About anything."

"You didn't have to," Kate said curtly. "I pay for your cell phone, your laptop. Do you think I can't see what you do every day?"

Claire physically recoiled, her eyes widening as she realized what was happening, that her mother had been spying on her.

"I know all about it," Kate said. "And enough is enough. Not only are you having an affair with a married man, but you brought him into my house."

Claire's mouth opened and closed as she tried to think of something to say.

"It doesn't matter," Kate said. "My issue isn't with you."

She turned her eyes back to Vince, the forty year old man who had been sleeping with a teenage girl. Feeling the rage building inside of her, Kate stepped toward him.

"You went after my daughter," Kate stated. "You pursued her until she relented. You purposefully went after a girl less than half your age. You went behind your wife's back. What kind of a man does that?"

He looked similar to Claire—his mouth opening and closing without any words coming out. The whole room was silent as Kate waited for a reply. She didn't get one. It was clear that Vince had nothing to say for himself. He knew it was wrong, there was no denying it.

"I should post this all over social media," Kate threatened. "I should tell your wife, your business partners, everyone around you. This little nugget of information would ruin your life, wouldn't it?"

Without missing a beat, Vince stepped out from behind the couch and stood opposite Kate, as if he were an equal. He looked down into her eyes and pressed his palms together.

"Listen," he said. "It's not what you think."

"So you are aware what you've done is wrong, then," Kate snapped. "Get out of my house. If I'm feeling generous, I won't put it on social media."

Vince gulped, the skin on his neck tightening as his Adam's apple bobbed up and down in his throat.

Kate knew that she was putting him in a hard position. She didn't much care. He had already ruined his life by getting involved with her daughter. It was his own fault. At least she was giving him a choice—coming clean on his own, or having some random woman expose him instead.

Vince gritted his teeth together and managed to rip his angry eyes away from Kate's face. He turned his head to Claire and his face softened. He reached out his hands for hers and, to Kate's horror, Claire reached out for him, too.

"Don't even think about it," Kate snapped. "If you ever *look* at my daughter the wrong way again, I will destroy you. You stay away from her and focus on your own life."

Vince retracted his hands, much to Claire's disdain. She cried out and slapped her hands over her mouth, stifling her sobs. Vince looked down to the floor and moved toward the front door, where he put on his shoes and prepared himself to leave. Kate watched his back until he was outside, closing the door on their lives forever.

"Mom!" Claire screamed. "How could you do this to me?"

Kate looked at her daughter as evenly as possible. "He was using you," she stated. "He's a creep. Do you think you're the first barely-legal girl he's gone after?"

Claire's face fell at those words. She looked out of the window, to where she could see Vince walking slowly down the driveway. She rushed to the door and opened it, screaming out his name. He turned around, tears in his eyes, and looked to Claire longingly.

"Is it true?" Claire called. "Am I not the first?"

Kate knew that Claire needed to hear this from the horse's mouth. She wasn't going to believe her mother, not after this huge scene. Kate stayed back and listened as Vince's shoes approached a couple of steps.

"I'm sorry," he said. "This was wrong. I'm wrong."

"Was I the first?" Claire screeched. "Did you lie to me?"

Kate couldn't hear a reply, but she knew that Claire had hers. A heart-breaking cry erupted out of her mouth, carrying down the street and echoing off the houses. Her baby's throat screamed out as her knees gave way, her body softly falling to the wood floor.

It was all very dramatic, Kate knew. But that's what life was like with teenagers. She grabbed her daughter and helped her up, closing the front door behind them.

The weekend passed Kate by painfully slowly. Claire had barely gotten out of bed, refusing to eat and drink as she sobbed her way to dehydration.

Kate kept an eye on her social media, and her phone usage, but nothing was being posted. No melodramatic posts, no calling out her mother, or her lover. Just radio silence. Kate was glad for that, at least.

The last thing Claire needed was fallout from idiotic posting on social media. She was trying to mend a broken heart.

Kate hadn't bothered calling Vince's wife. She had enough to deal with. Not only did she have a melancholy teen but she also had to get ready to go back to work. The war at home had been won with casualties; she didn't want the same to happen at the office. She'd had enough drama for a lifetime.

Preparing for work while her daughter sobbed upstairs was tough, but somehow Kate pulled through. She read through all the emails and got through everything she'd missed.

After a couple of phone calls to good friends in her department, finding out what people had been saying about her behind her back, Kate was caught up completely.

There was nothing that could surprise her on her return. She'd even prepared for the worst—for getting to work and being called into her boss's office and being fired immediately.

Kate went to bed early on Sunday night and found herself wide awake at six in the morning on Monday. She got ready slowly, choosing her clothes carefully, and got back into the routine with ease.

Before she knew it, she was standing outside the building of her corporate office, with her bag slung over her shoulder, with her project files and laptop tucked away inside.

She took a deep, steadying breath as she looked up at the building. Everyone who wanted her fired was inside, as well as everyone who had her back. It was going to feel awful when she stepped in there, feeling everyone's eyes on her, but she knew it would be like a band-aid: rip it off quick and it'll hurt way less.

That's exactly what she did. Kate held her head up high and straightened her back before storming into the office like the boss that she was. She wore her fears like armor, reminding herself that even if her worst fears were realized, they still wouldn't be able to hurt her. She could find another job somewhere else, a place where they'd appreciate her worth.

As soon as she walked through the lobby, the receptionist's eyes snapped to hers. She stood up from behind the desk, putting the phone against her shoulder, muffling the microphone, as she tried to wave down Kate.

"Kate!" she called. "Kate! You need to wait!"

There was no plausible reason that Kate could see. She worked here. She was one of the most senior members of the company. Why the hell should she wait for anyone?

Instead of doing as she was told, she ignored the receptionist and strolled right past her, heading for the elevators. Nothing in the world could have stopped her. She was going to give this presentation and she was going to own it.

Kate walked through the office, between the desks, with her head held high. She could feel everyone moving around to stare at her but instead of making her feel insecure, it just made her more confident.

They weren't staring at her maliciously, or because she needed to be stared at, but because she was walking through the office without giving a single fuck to what anyone else thought. Who wouldn't marvel at that?

At the end of the room, she could see her favorite group of men piling into the conference room, about to start their Monday meeting. Kate hurried her pace to catch them before they closed the door, but she wasn't quick enough. They closed her out, probably trying to keep her out of their way for a while longer.

Kate wasn't going to accept that, though. She swung the door open and stepped inside. All of the chatter instantly stopped. A couple of men rose from the desks and pointed their fingers at the door, shouting at her to get out.

"Oh, do shut up," Kate sighed, rolling her eyes as she slipped her bag off her shoulder. "I have as much of a right to be here as any of you."

When she set her bag on the table, she saw her boss sitting to the left of her, his translucent hair looking terribly thin. She looked down at Walter Harpe and put one of her hands on her hips.

"How about we try this again?" Kate asked. "I'll give my presentation, you'll all listen, and we can move on."

"You need to leave!" One of the men screamed from the back.

Kate turned to look at him, her eyes dead and cold. She stared at him until he paled and sat back down in his seat, thoroughly afraid for his life.

"Kate," Walter moaned. "We don't have time to listen to you."

"And yet you have time to listen to every other person in this room," Kate snapped. "How very sexist of you."

She looked around at every pair of eyes in the room, feeling the confidence ooze out of her whole body. There was no stopping her, not now. She was on a roll and she wasn't going to let these withered old men get in her way.

"No," Kate sighed, letting herself smile widely. "You were all incredibly rude to me last time I was in this office. You're all going to apologize and listen to my presentation like you should have the first time around instead of sending me off on a forced absence."

Most of the men stared down at the table, their cheeks blushing pink as they were called out for their nonsense. Walter Harpe gritted his teeth together but said nothing. Instead, he leaned back in his chair.

Kate would have seen that as a sign of permission before but now she knew that she didn't need his permission. She was in this position for a reason—she was good at what she did—and she deserved their professional respect.

It only took her a second to open up her laptop and plug it into the projector. When her papers were beside the laptop on the desk in front of her, she straightened her suit jacket and looked around the room slowly, making sure to make eye contact with every man there, staring them down to show dominance.

"Thank you," she smiled. "Now, let's begin."

Author's Note

Do men roll their eyes at you? Do they call you sweetheart and treat you like a spoiled little girl? Do they stare at your tits instead of paying attention to your face?

If so, it means they don't take you seriously.

Wanna know why?

Because you're not assertive enough.

And there's no better way to become more assertive than to take a two-week vacation in a tropical resort where you get fucked and fucked and fucked by a bunch of hunky young men who are all begging for your attention and are eager to do every damn thing you order them to.

Is there?

And yeah, I know it's demeaning to the guys. Bossing them around, humiliating them. But how else are they supposed to learn? They need someone to teach them, and that someone is you.

Besides, by teaching them to be more attentive to your needs, you're doing them a huge favor. You're helping them become better lovers.

And, when all is said and done, you can wash your hands of it all, go back home and take charge of your life. Show the men who is boss.

I understand, of course, that sometimes *you* want to be the one being dominated.

You want to be made to submit. By a strong man who truly deserves your submission.

Well, if that's the case, I want you to read my book *Dangerous Desires*.

Dangerous Desires is a forbidden romance involving an older woman and a savage younger man who knows what he wants and won't let anything stop him from getting it.

If that's the kind of thing you're into, read *Dangerous Desires* now.

And if you want a full range of steamy scenarios, check out my free book *Dirty Confessions*.

Love,
Viktor

Bonus chapter

Excerpt from the book* Dangerous Desires *by Viktor Redreich

Birgitta gulped and turned off the tap, keeping her eyes on the door. She felt the droplets of water falling away from her face but made no effort to wipe them away. They fell down to her chest and shoulders, causing ripples of goosebumps to spread across her skin.

"Gitta," Micah mumbled through the door.

Birgitta opened her mouth to tell him to go away but immediately closed it. She knew it was a ridiculous idea, but hoped that if she stayed quiet he would just go away.

"Gitta, I know you're in there," he said. "You can't keep avoiding me."

"I'm in the bathroom," Birgitta stated.

It was the only answer she could come up with. Of course, she was in the bathroom—he was talking to her *through the door.* Even though it was stupid, it worked. She heard his footsteps trailing away into the kitchen.

Birgitta could finally breathe again. Her hand clutched the lip of the sink as her head started to spin.

What the hell am I going to do? She thought. *I can't keep living like this. I can't be a prisoner in my own home.*

Birgitta didn't think about what she was doing as she moved to the bathroom door and unlocked it. She threw the door open and walk toward the kitchen. The door bashed against the wall loudly, no doubt startling Micah. Birgitta rounded into the kitchen and saw Micah's back facing her.

"I want you," she said, the words pouring out of her mouth so quickly they turned into a jumbled mess. "Now."

Micah spun around and looked at her, startled and confused. "Now?"

Birgitta felt the chill in the air against her skin. She wanted to glance down at herself, but she knew what she was wearing—almost nothing, a slinky little dress that barely covered her thighs, with a robe wrapped loosely around her shoulders. How could Micah resist her, when she looked like that? She was basically naked already, ripe for the taking.

Micah seized the opportunity, as she'd expected. As he walked across the kitchen, his socks slipped on the shining floor. It didn't make his stride slow, though. He stormed until her body was wrapped tightly in her arms.

Birgitta was almost thrown backward from the weight of his body smashing into hers. His arms wound around her back, his hands tangling into her hair. Birgitta felt her body go limp as she sank into him. Their lips were pressed together tightly, their tongues dancing. She could feel her body melting into his, merging until they were just one.

Somehow, Birgitta found herself perched on the edge of the counter, where Micah had been standing before. The cupboard handles were digging into her back. Her legs wrapped around Micah's waist instinctively, drawing his pelvis tight against hers.

She could feel the warmth spreading up her body from her sex, making every inch of her body burn. The only thing she wanted at that moment was to touch every piece of Micah's body. Her hand went down to the front of his pants. Birgitta's fingertips peeled away the elastic waistband. She hadn't realized he was wearing sweats, too distracted by him to pay attention to his clothes.

All it meant was she had easy access to his cock. She peeled the waistband from his body and let her hand sink down beneath the fabric. His cock was growing with every second that passed. She could feel it beneath his underwear, hard and warm. Birgitta let her fingers slide up and down the shaft. In reply, Micah moved his lips down to her neck and began sucking at the tender skin there.

Birgitta gasped as a shudder rolled through her body, taking control of her. She could feel a trail of saliva down her neck, like a line of breadcrumbs showing where Micah had been. Her hand didn't stop moving, gently caressing him until his cock was bursting out of his pants.

When he was ready, his hands planted on Birgitta's thighs. His hands moved upward, his fingers ready to hook into her underwear and pull it down. Birgitta smiled into their kiss as he realized that she wasn't wearing any underwear. Within a second his fingers had slipped inside her, exploring her soaking wet hole.

Birgitta lost all control of her body then. Her head leaned back into the cupboards and her mouth fell open. Short, breathless sounds left her mouth but even she didn't know what they were supposed to mean. Having Micah inside her—even if it was just his fingers—was better than she could have ever imagined. He kept pushing deeper and deeper until her legs were spread wide apart.

With his thumb pressed on her clitoris, he began to press against her. Birgitta's breath caught in her throat, and her hands clamped down on his arms, her nails digging into his muscles.

It wasn't enough for her, though. She needed to know what it would feel like to have his cock in her mouth, to have it plunging deep inside her soaked pussy. Birgitta broke away the kiss and held Micah's face between her hands.

He was frowning as he worked her, his whole right arm shaking as he tried to please her. Birgitta grabbed his face tighter, drawing his attention away from her body. His deep brown eyes looked into her blue. They stopped, both perfectly still, as they stared at one another.

The moment was broken by the sounds of tires crunching against the gravel driveway. Birgitta's heart felt like it was going to explode as the rush of adrenaline pumped through her body. Without thinking, she shoved Micah's hands away from her, causing his fingers to withdraw from between her legs. She instantly lowered herself off the counter and adjusted her gown, tugging it down to cover her body before wrapping the robe tightly around herself, covering every inch of her body from the neck to her calves.

"What's your problem?" Micah asked, the frustration clear in his angry voice.

"He can't see us," Birgitta snapped. "He can't know."

What to read next

Read Now

books2read.com/DangerousDesires

Also by Viktor Redreich

Innocence Corrupted Collection

Trixie Provoked

Sophie Corrupted

Megan Disgraced

Amber Stigmatized

Cindy Violated

Kelly Exposed

Savage Satisfactions Collection

Submissive Nanny

Hunky Neighbor

Blushing Maid

Risky Mistress

Jealous Wife

Demanding Husband

Desires Unleashed Collection

Dangerous Desires

Indecent Temptations

Explicit Demands

Sordid Fixations

Illicit Compulsions

Shameful Addictions

Books can be read in any order

Get your free copy of Dirty Secrets

Elyse said that she's been secretly letting a young man fuck her. He's her massage therapist and he was supposed to keep it professional but his hands kept wandering under the towel and touching her in places he *shouldn't* have been touching her.

One thing led to another and pretty soon he just peeled off his clothes. Fit body completely exposed to her, he climbed up on top of her, pushed her legs apart, and penetrated her.

Elyse isn't the only one having fun with younger men. Nicole is too.

In fact, Nicole told me that the college guy who lives next door to her has been watching her sunbathe in her bikini by the pool. At first, she was angry about him staring at her from his upstairs bedroom window. Soon though, she started to enjoy the attention.

Last I heard she even took her top off and rubbed lotion on her titties for him to watch.

Oh and you who else is behaving scandalously? Miranda.

Miranda's husband is a hunk and their sex life is great. She heard her husband bragging to one of his friends about how good and sexy Miranda is. How willing and eager she is. How she's basically up for anything.

Then out of nowhere Miranda's husband told her to suck his friend's dick.

Do you think that's going too far?

I think they're *all* going too far. Elyse, Nicole *and* Miranda.

What shocks me is how eager they were to tell me these things. How much detail they went into.

They really opened up to me. They literally told me *everything.*

Being a writer, I wrote it all down. Every dirty detail. All of Miranda's, Nicole's, and Elyse's secrets, plus the secrets of many other women just like them.

Just like *you*.

Get your free book now

Redreich.com/DirtySecrets/

www.ingramcontent.com/pod-product-compliance
Lightning Source LLC
La Vergne TN
LVHW012049160826
845678LV00014B/2755

* 9 7 8 1 9 1 3 3 7 6 2 5 3 *